NOTHING WILL BE LEFT

The Quill Point Chronicles 1

Nothing Will Be Left

October Kane

4 Horsemen Publications, Inc.

1497 Main St. Suite 169
Dunedin, FL 34698
4horsemenpublications.com
info@4horsemenpublications.com

Cover and Typesetting by Niki Tantillo
Edited by Kristine Cotter

Library of Congress Control Number: 2022951293
Paperback ISBN-13: 978-1-64450-746-9
Hardcover ISBN-13: 978-1-64450-747-6
Audiobook ISBN-13: 978-1-64450-749-0
Ebook ISBN-13: 978-1-64450-748-3

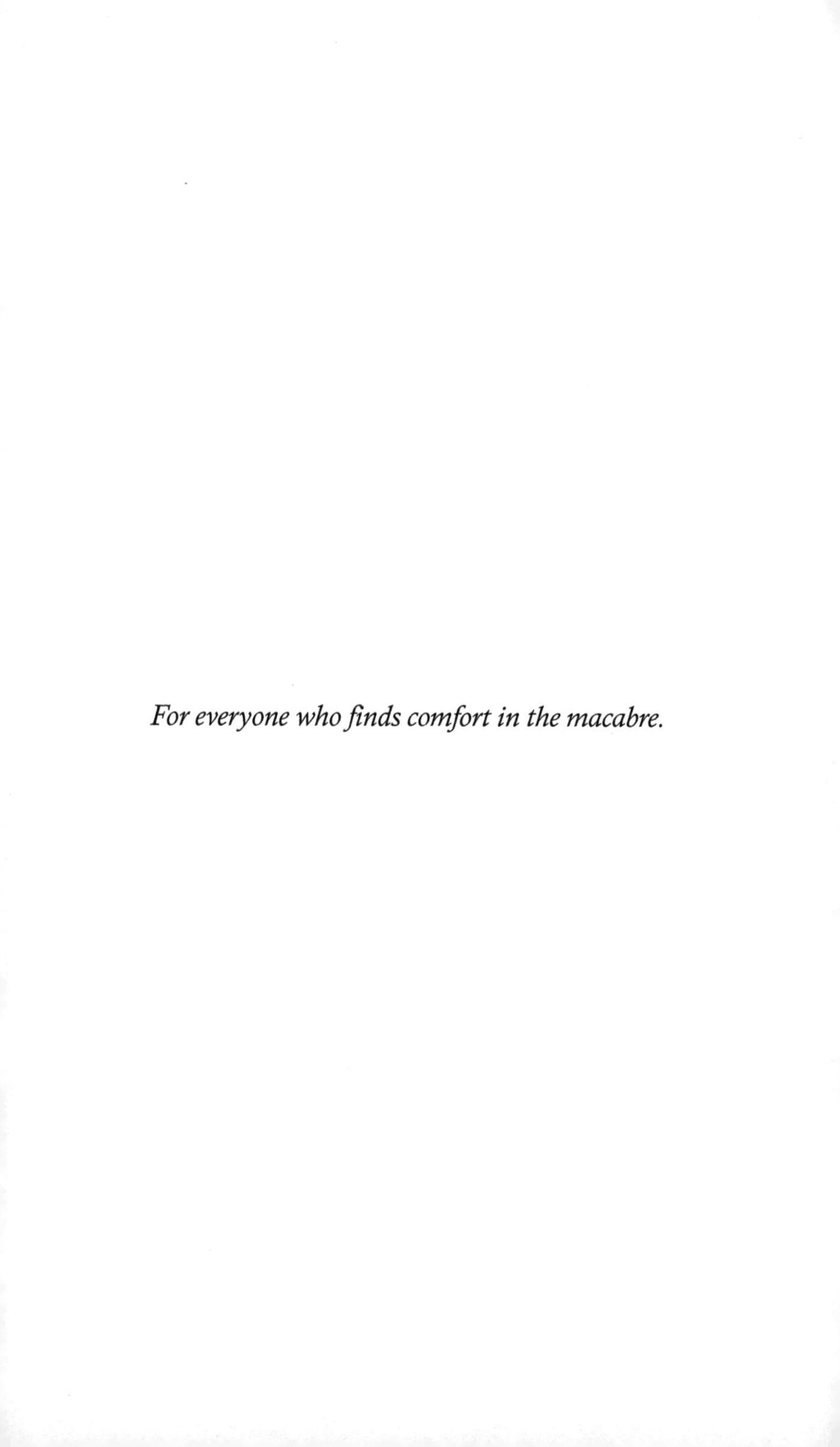

For everyone who finds comfort in the macabre.

Acknowledgments

Despite popular myths, most books are not just one person's efforts. Sure, I wrote *Nothing Will Be Left*, but it wouldn't exist without so many people helping me along the way. I want to thank my early readers, my editor, and everyone at 4 Horsemen Publications who helped make this possible. I've spent hundreds of hours daydreaming about this series, and I can hardly believe the first book is real.

Table of Contents

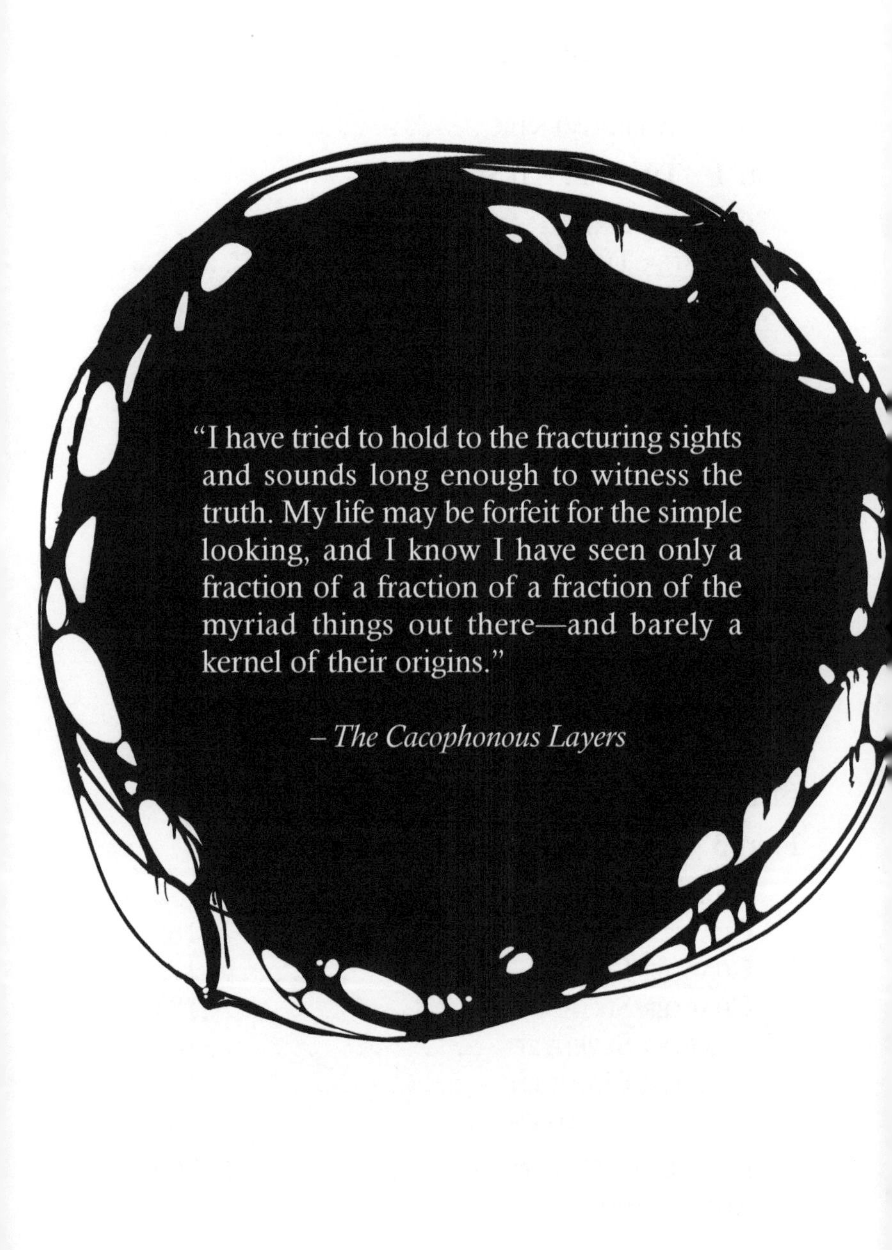

"I have tried to hold to the fracturing sights and sounds long enough to witness the truth. My life may be forfeit for the simple looking, and I know I have seen only a fraction of a fraction of a fraction of the myriad things out there—and barely a kernel of their origins."

– The Cacophonous Layers

Part 1
The Warped Sky

Chapter One

ALBERT HADN'T EVEN INTENDED TO BE IN Quill Point, Illinois, when everything started. He had planned to leave the day prior. The only reason he was still in town was that his clunker of a car had stopped working.

Not that he hated Quill Point, just that it was boring. The only thing to do after nine o'clock was to go to the inexplicably still surviving roller rink. It was the kind of small town made for retirees, not someone in their mid-twenties. He was pretty sure that growing up here was the whole reason he'd felt compelled to leave for the bustle of California.

He'd caught up with his parents as best he could, but there wasn't that much to catch up on. They'd never met his girlfriend before the breakup. Neither of his parents knew enough about software and coding to truly get what he did at work. It was nothing but dead-end conversations.

So, mid-afternoon on a warm Thursday, he found himself walking to the cluster of restaurants near the highway access ramp.

A free-standing coffee shop seemed the most interesting. It had been a long time since he'd gone to anything other than a chain. His apartment was next to quite a few franchises, and they all knew his orders.

As he walked across the blacktop, the wind changed. A breeze turned to a cold burst. Albert's blazer whipped around him.

He turned to look, frowning. A storm cloud was rolling in from the eastern horizon. It wasn't like anything he'd heard of in Quill Point before. Illinois had tornado season, but this looked like a tropical storm.

It was far away, though. No raindrops, no thunder. The only thing that changed was the temperature. The clouds heralded a drop of almost ten degrees. It went from summer warmth to a fall chill.

With every step, the coffee shop seemed more appealing. Albert pulled the blazer around himself and walked faster. He kept looking at the clouds, expecting them to burst with lightning at any moment. Bells chimed when he opened the door to the Quill Point Café. The barista looked up as he entered and didn't hide her befuddled look. Albert had been getting a lot of those since he'd been in Quill Point. He was an unfamiliar face in a routine that was older than him.

"Hey there." The barista was short and small, with mildly tanned white skin, not-quite gray hair, and seemed maybe in her early sixties. "Haven't seen you before."

"I'm Georgina's kid," Albert replied automatically.

The woman's face lit up.

"Oh, well, of course you are," she said with a faint Chicagoan accent. "You look so much like her. You even have your mother's black hair, now, don't you?"

"Yeah, and my father's gray eyes," Albert said.

"Such a small world. I think I saw you once or twice as a toddler." She smiled with her eyes as much as her mouth. "Well, my name's Cynthia. What can I get for you?"

"Something warm," Albert said. "Cold spell just came in."

Cynthia pursed her lips slightly. "That so? That's weird. Well, the menu's up there—just tell me what you'd like."

Albert looked. It was drawn in dark blue chalk on a chalkboard suspended above the counter. The fare was the usual: espresso, latte, some sugary stuff—except for a "Mug of Ink," which didn't even have a list of ingredients.

"Ah, I see my special concoction has caught your eye."

"Yeah, it has," Albert said. "What is it, exactly?"

"Oh, it's something for the busy people. I know a lawyer who swears by it. It's my wife's concoction—she's never been much of a morning person."

Albert looked over the name again as though it would reveal its secrets. He was no slouch when it came to caffeine. Coming out of college, he'd chugged enough energy drinks to rot his insides.

"What's in it?" he asked.

Cynthia smiled mischievously. "Well, the better question is, what's not in it? Would you like a free cup? Got to get you hooked on the stuff, after all."

Albert made a small sound in the back of his throat. "Uh, I still think I want to know what I'm drinking."

"Well, I can't tell you everything, but it's mostly ristretto and dark chocolate syrup. I recommend you sip it slowly. Unless you want to live on the moon the next time you jump."

"Uh … sure, I'll try it." Albert let out a little breath. "Sure, may as well. I have a lot more walking to do today."

"That a fact?" Cynthia said. When she took out a bag of beans from behind the counter and loaded it into the machine, Albert wondered if his order was a good idea.

"Yeah, I've been looking around the town, seeing how the place is."

A soft bell sounded behind him. Albert turned to see an older man stepping into the store. He had dark brown skin, a pale beard dominating most of his lower jaw, and noticeable laugh lines. He used a roller and was also holding a leash. His dog strained against it, sniffing at Albert's leg. Albert wasn't great at identifying breeds of dogs, but it was small, fluffy, and blond, with a tiny pink tongue lapping at the air.

"Some weather out there," the man said.

"Hey there, Henry. How have you and Saanvi been?" Cynthia called from behind the counter. She'd started the espresso machine, filling three small metal cups with ristretto.

"Somehow, someway, that wife of mine gets more gorgeous every year. So, I can't complain. I came by to get the household some beans for the mornings—we're getting low. I thought I'd get some before dark. I guess I was psychic with my timing. Those clouds look ready for rain."

Albert frowned at that. The dog still followed him as he walked to the café's closest window. His eyes went wide. The sky had gotten wilder. The clouds were much closer. Colors were leaking along their edge. Ribbons of orange and red spread from them like streamers. Something about it made his pulse quicken. It reminded him of a poisonous frog.

"Is that normal here?" Albert asked.

"Not anything I've seen," Henry replied.

Henry's dog made a small whine and backed away from the window. The noise made the hairs on Albert's neck stand up straight.

Cynthia walked over to stand next to him. She took one look and whistled.

"That's one heck of a thing."

As if it could hear her, the clouds finally released a deep purple lightning bolt. It was massive, forking into several stabbing points. No thunder came yet, but it made Albert blink. The afterimage stayed in his vision for several seconds.

"I think maybe I need to get home." Albert's voice was quieter than he expected. His legs felt weak.

"Didn't you say you were walking?" Cynthia asked.

His stomach dropped. "Uh … yeah, I did."

Cynthia frowned slightly. "Hey, Henry, mind giving this boy a ride to his parents'?"

"That depends," Henry said, walking over. "Who is this mystery person?"

"This here is Georgina and Terry's kid, Albert. He's here for some reason—hadn't told me yet."

"Uh, hi," Albert said, tearing his eyes away from the storm cloud. It was widening now. Spreading the length of his peripheral vision. "…I'm just visiting."

A faint rumbling of thunder came from seemingly everywhere at once. The dog whimpered again, and Cynthia dropped to hold him. Henry nodded to her before looking Albert over.

"Hello, Albert. I've known your parents for a few years now. They've always been good people. I can give you a ride if you don't mind me getting what I came for first."

"The usual, I assume?" Cynthia said, still patting the dog on the head. When the dog stopped visibly tensing, she stood up and returned to the counter.

"If you have it," Henry said. "It's the best thing I've had."

"I appreciate the flattery," she said, "but I've had it as fresh as possible—the day after it was roasted—and you can't even imagine."

"I bet." Henry turned back to Albert. "Are you okay with waiting?"

Albert nodded, even if some part of him wanted to run, as fast as he could, for the nearest house. He felt somehow cornered. Another rumble off in the distance made his shoulder twitch.

"Your drink's ready, hun," Cynthia said. "Though you're starting to look like you don't need any more energy."

"Sorry," Albert said. "I'm not sure what came over me there. I'm not usually bothered by storms."

"It does look really nasty," Cynthia said.

Albert nodded in agreement and picked up the ceramic mug set out on the counter. It was heavy and full of a thick black liquid that slightly stained the edge of the cup. After a second of trepidation, he took a sip. He was too nervous to enjoy it, but it had the same quality as wine with its oddly unfolding flavors. It was also quite strong and made his head buzz.

"Oh, that stuff will kill you," Henry joked. "I had one ten years ago—and I think it's still making it hard for me to sleep."

"Now, don't go scaring off my customers," Cynthia said.

"I like it," Albert muttered, glancing out the window.

Cynthia handed a dark gray bag to Henry. He took it with a smile and a nod. After paying, he turned back to Albert.

"So, then, let's get you home. Will you be okay with me stopping by and saying hello to your folks? Or is there a family dinner planned I'd be interrupting?"

"You can do that. It's fine. I just—I want to not be here when whatever this is hits."

Henry looked out the window. For a moment, a bright purple light washed over his face. A flash of concern came and went, but he still smiled at Albert.

"All right, my car's just out here." He waved to Cynthia as he turned to leave, letting in the cold as he opened the door. "Thanks for the coffee! Tell your wife we should play some cards again sometime."

"She'll win, you know," Cynthia replied.

"Well, naturally, but it's still fun."

Albert took one more sip of his coffee and put the mug back on the counter. "Sorry I couldn't finish it. It was good. I liked it."

"Oh, don't worry about it. But come back before you go back to your fancy town, okay? It's always nice seeing the new generation become adults."

"Thanks, I … I will," Albert said.

"Don't worry too much about the weather," Cynthia said. "We get some strange days. It once rained for almost a week. And you should've seen the snow in nineteen sixty-seven."

"Okay, thanks," Albert said. "You … be safe, too."

Cynthia nodded. "I will be. Worse comes to worst, I'll throw some tarp over the windows and go to the bigger shops. They can take a few hits."

"Okay, good," Albert said.

When he turned, Henry was finishing getting himself, his roller, and his dog into his car. He waved from the front seat. The car was a sturdy thing—old but well-built. Albert knew little about cars, but it had large headlights and a flat front.

The wind whipped at him, yet again, during the brief trip to the car. He opened the passenger door, and within seconds of sitting down, the dog leaped over and sniffed at his chest.

Henry laughed. "That's Buddy. Sorry about him. He's usually a little more well-behaved."

"It's okay. I like dogs," Albert replied.

He adjusted so Buddy could better sit on his lap. Buddy seemed dead set on licking Albert's palms, no matter where he put his hands. He forgot about the storm outside for a second, but another rumble made him look out the window.

Any other thoughts left him. The clouds and the sky were like nothing he'd ever imagined. The large gray storm clouds were in every direction. They made a ring of the horizon, surrounding the town. The red and orange ribbons leaked out even further.

"That's a wild thing," Henry muttered, then started the car.

"This is impossible," Albert said.

Something tightened in the pit of his stomach. He took out his phone and pointed the camera at it. Only after he took a picture did he notice that his hand was shaking.

"You might want to send that to the weather station," Henry said quietly. He sounded nervous now. "They'd probably love some on-the-ground footage."

Buddy softly growled on Albert's lap. The sound started a spark of panic that Albert had to swallow back down. The car felt too small, and the sky was far too big.

"Sure, uh, what's the number?"

Henry told him as they exited the parking lot. It took only a few minutes to get back to his parents' place, and he spent nearly all of it trying to input the number. The shaking in his hand and the thrumming in his chest made it hard to type. He kept starting over when he got a number wrong.

He got it about two blocks from his house. His phone immediately told him he didn't have service. He tried again. It didn't work.

"Is there a cell tower nearby?" Albert asked.

"Yeah, the town didn't like it, but we have one about a mile from here."

"Ah, okay," Albert said. "The connection's not good."

"This is going to be a big storm," Henry said. "I think there might be a tornado coming or something."

The sky had become almost entirely that orange and red color. Only the faintest hints of blue remained, and even the sunlight streaming down seemed altered.

Henry's hands tightened on the steering wheel. "I'll have to take a rain check on seeing your folks, Albert. I think I want to get home."

"That's fine," Albert said. "Just pull over here; I can walk the last bit."

Henry nodded slowly. There were barely any cars on the road, so he quickly pulled off to the side. He gave Albert a strained smile. "Stay safe, okay?"

"Thanks." Albert eased Buddy off of him and opened the car door. "Thanks for the ride."

"Welcome," Henry said, staring out the driver's side window.

As soon as Albert closed the car door, Henry peeled away. His car picked up speed as he rounded the corner.

Albert looked up again as it happened: a purple bolt segmented overhead, and a frigid wind shot around him. The sky was bloated with orange. It looked as if he could stretch to his tiptoes, reach out, and come back with stained hands.

Something deep in Albert's chest vibrated. It kept shuddering. He touched his chest. His heart rate had never been this fast before.

He didn't stop to think. Albert ran for his parents' place. Another rumble vibrated the air. It made his stomach shudder. He panted, pushing his feet to carry him a little more.

There was a flash so bright Albert had to blink it away. The resulting thunderclap came less than a second later. It slapped the air above his head.

It set off multiple car alarms.

Albert's parents' house came into view, and he picked up more speed. In the warped light, the squat building looked different. Hedges that sat below the windows shivered. The wind chimes hanging from the eaves spun and jumped and screeched.

Another roll of thunder happened, but didn't stop booming. It seemed to move down into the ground, digging its fingers at the very earth. Albert stumbled. He felt like he was on uneven ground. He stopped in his tracks, and the ground was still moving; he was still shaking.

Albert had felt earthquakes in California.

This was something else.

The ground shifted like the tide. Everything he could see, everywhere he could feel, was atop a striding horse, bucking him up and down.

The sky burst with another lightning strike. It also didn't stop. Bolts crackled and split the air. The thunder somehow got even louder. Albert cupped his hands over his ears and cowered. He was possibly shouting, possibly crying. He couldn't hear himself.

In the rolling chaos, he wasn't even sure he could locate his own body. It felt, it shivered, but it was so small compared to the yawning void of wind.

Albert stumbled again, then fell hard. The world seemed to split, break, and unravel. The ground rose to smash into his side. A scream burst out from his lips. He was sure he was crying now. He was not sure of anything else.

The moments that followed seemed endless. Albert lost track of time as he lay there, shirking away from the buffeting cold, roaring thunder, and angry earth below. His only want was for it to stop.

When it finally did, when the fury of the elements lessened and then ceased, he didn't notice at first. He had fled to some part of himself, some deep part of his mind, and had grown numb. It took moments of mounting soreness, of awareness of the dirt coating his arms, to find himself again. He flexed his fingers, and they hurt from how hard he'd tightened them into fists.

He didn't want to open his eyes. The devastation around him was a sight he wasn't sure he could handle.

But then he heard his mother's panicked voice, and his mind slammed fully back into the world. His eyes shot open. Everything was foggy and full of floaters. Albert pushed himself into a sitting position.

He wasn't in the center of a singed crater, but the damage was everywhere. Trees toppled. The pavement had deep cracks in it. Mailboxes lay unearthed in the road.

It was oddly silent, though. The car alarms had stopped.

With all Albert's willpower, he looked up again.

The sky was pure red and orange, the blue gone. The storm clouds encircled the sky, gray and solid. They didn't shoot out any more lightning, but they hadn't gotten any smaller.

Albert's mom cried out again. With what little energy he had left, Albert stumbled to stand. With pain from every step, he walked as quickly as he could to his parents' front door.

Chapter Two

When Albert reached the door, his legs almost failed him. He buckled forward, crashing into the wood with a grunt. He leaned there for a moment. His muscles were sore. His body was tense and yet too loose to function. It was hard to think clearly.

"Hello!" his mother called from behind the door. "Someone, please help us!"

Albert wobbled, but found enough stability to pull on the door handle. It didn't fully open. The frame had shifted slightly off. He had to squeeze through the narrow gap. He stumbled into the house and paused after a few steps. The inside of his parents' house was in ruins.

A bookcase full of large novels had fallen on its side and partially blocked the pathway. The broken sections of wood jutted in various directions. Several books lay open, splayed out on their spines.

A vase he could recall being in the background in a picture of his first actual date with his first actual girlfriend was chunks of blue across the floor. A couch he'd fallen asleep on after the only soccer game he'd ever played was tilting to the side on snapped legs.

"I'm here, I'm here," he yelled into the house.

"Albert?! Oh, thank god you're okay. Come here. Your father—he's unconscious."

Albert stumbled deeper into the house, stepping over piles of broken glass from several fallen picture frames. He barely avoided crushing his own younger face.

Albert turned a corner to find his mother straining to hold up a fallen shelf. Her jet-black hair was wild, and her shirt was covered in dust. She was panting so hard that it sounded like she was on the verge of passing out. Her beige complexion was flushing from the strain. Books lay in piles around his father—some looked quite heavy.

Another surge of adrenaline hit Albert, and he moved to help. The sharp wood bit into his hand. Together, the two lifted it off further and then to the side, letting it crash down on the carpet with a thud.

"Is he okay?" Albert dropped down to his father. As far as he could see, his father was still breathing. He had a nasty bruise on the side of his head.

"I think so ... I don't know..." his mother said breathlessly. She was wringing her hands now, her eyes wide and her mouth in a tight line. "It hit him, and he stopped talking."

"Where is the hospital in this town?" Albert asked.

"Um." His mom looked around at nothing. For a second, it was like her mind had simply fled. She took a shaky breath. "Yeah, yeah, it's like five miles away."

"Okay," Albert said.

His mother frowned and was clearly fighting tears.

"Dad?" Albert said softly. He put his hand gingerly against his father's cheek. Albert's dad had pale white skin to begin with, but now he looked sickly. Albert was worried that if his dad had a concussion, or something similar, he would only make it worse if he used too much force.

"Hey, Dad, can you wake up?"

A slow groan escaped his father's lips, his eyelids fluttered gently. After another slightly louder grunt, his eyes opened, but his pupils were unfocused. He blinked a few times.

"What happened?" he said. "I don't..."

"You hit your head, Dad," Albert said.

"I... what happened? It was so loud. Did a tornado hit?"

"I don't know what it was," Albert said. "The sky outside looks wrong."

He turned back to his mother. "Can you call an ambulance?"

"I need a ... I..."

His father groaned again, then started puking. It mainly was retching; little came from his lips. Albert shuddered along with him, holding him as the wracking heaves hit.

"Okay," his mother muttered and walked out of the room.

"It's okay, Dad." Albert held his hand as he finished vomiting. "We'll get you some help."

"Thanks," his dad said sleepily.

"There's no connection," his mom said behind him. Her voice sounded wrong. It was hollow, shaky, and full of something Albert had never heard from his mother before.

"Okay." Albert nearly lost his own words—almost unable to speak. "Let me try mine."

The indicators weren't there. His phone displayed no nearby internet connections and had no noticeable signal. He tried to call emergency services. His phone didn't even ring.

"I guess the ... I guess whatever happened knocked out the cell tower. Or something."

"Let's get him to the car," his mother said.

Albert nodded. He let out a long breath. "Dad, I'm going to move you. We'll do it slowly, and I'll not bump you, but you need to stay as still as you can, okay?"

His dad made a sound that could be considered agreement. Albert winced, but moved to prepare. The first aid and emergency training he'd gotten in high school rose in his mind. He recalled, vaguely, that you could use a blanket to drag a person.

Albert stepped to grab a large brown and orange blanket lying across the back of a chair ... but then paused. He couldn't recall what he needed to do and couldn't search for answers online.

After a moment, he just put his arms underneath his father's and tried to tug him upward to stand. Albert's body screamed at him. All the soreness flooded his limbs, crashing against his mind. His dad made another grunting sound, a wobbly thing coming from somewhere in his throat. Albert almost screamed out as he strained, but he got his father to a standing position.

"Okay, let's just get him to the car," Albert said once he could breathe properly.

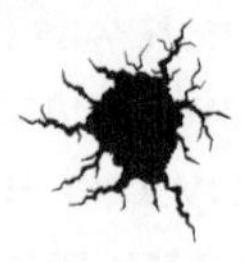

Seeing it again was as jarring as it had been the first time. The sky blazed that strange alien orange, stained with red.

The storm clouds glowed with their uncast lightning, but remained silent.

"What in god's name?" his mother whispered.

"Was it a nuke?" his dad muttered. "I knew ... someday it would happen."

Albert just gently shook his head. The way it had happened, even with the boom and the vibrations, didn't feel like what he assumed a nuke going off would feel like. There wasn't any heat; there wasn't anything centralized. It had felt like it came from the earth below and stars above and from the depth and limits of the world.

He kept taking his father to the car. There wasn't much discussion about driving: his mother got into the seat and put the keys in. She tried to start it a few times.

And then a few more.

The engine would give out a progressively weaker sputter each time she turned the key. It grew to a faint rumble and a whine. She pulled out the keys, put them back in, and turned it so hard Albert could see her knuckles go white.

Tears flowed down her face gently, with no sound. Albert felt something bubble in his chest and shake at his bones. He wanted to scream out in frustration, but all that came out of his mouth was a tense, shaky breath.

"Okay, so, cars don't work, the phone doesn't work..."

He looked up and down the street, trying to find something—he wasn't sure what it even could be. He didn't know how to fix a car. Didn't know how to administer medical aid.

Albert was about to panic when he saw something useful: other people. In small clusters, they walked along the sidewalk. Some were bleeding from shallow wounds; some looked truly exhausted.

Albert got out of the car as one of the few familiar faces came up alongside the house. Henry walked slowly alongside a woman with light-brown skin, gray hair, and large rectangular glasses. She was holding Buddy's leash.

Albert took a few shaky steps toward the two. The panic in his chest loosened a little at seeing Henry okay. Even the crowds of faces he didn't know were reassuring. So many people alive, if seriously shaken, was a miracle.

"Henry!" he called out, his voice catching slightly.

Henry looked over; it was like he'd escaped a bad dream. His frown slightly faded. "Hey there! I see your folks and you are okay. Thank god. I don't ... I don't know what happened."

"Are you okay?" Albert asked.

Henry let out a small breath. "A little shaken up is all. The house is fine, but a tree came *this* close."

"Hi, Henry told me about you," said the woman beside him. "I'm glad to see you're okay."

"A bookshelf fell on my dad," Albert said. The words felt acidic coming out of his mouth. "We should get him to the hospital, but..."

"The cars aren't working," Henry said, his voice heavy. "Whatever's happening, it's making things not function anymore. I'm not sure the hospital will be any better right now. The lights are staying on, but that's no guarantee. I ... hope everyone's okay."

Albert looked back at his house for a second. He'd not paid attention to it, but Henry was right. There had still been light. The air conditioning and ceiling fans had been working. His cell and the car didn't work, but the lights still did. A nearby streetlight had even activated as it got closer to sundown.

"Where are you going?" Albert asked. The people he saw walking by were heading in the same direction.

"In an emergency," Henry explained, "protocol is to meet in the middle of the town. Go to the town center. It's just an emergency plan in case of a tornado or something. The walls there are the best. Though that doesn't matter now."

"You should come with," Henry's wife said. "A doctor might be there for your father."

"Thanks, uh..."

"Saanvi," she said. "And you're welcome."

"This town's been through a lot in its history," Henry said. "I don't know what's happening, though. I've never seen..."

He looked up at the sky and bit his lip. That frown slipped into place, and he seemed a million miles away. When he didn't talk for another moment, Saanvi patted him on the shoulder.

Henry looked back at her and smiled, albeit faintly.

"It's going to be okay," Saanvi said. A crinkle passed across her lips. A tightening of her jaw. "I'm sure we'll figure something out."

Albert's father groaned again, and Albert looked back in alarm. His mom was barely keeping him standing.

"I'm not sure a walk will be possible," Albert said.

"Oh... of course," Saanvi began. "I'm sure we can find someone to help with that."

"Thanks," Albert replied.

"This town *will* get through it, okay?"

"...okay."

Saanvi nodded. Albert nodded back and then walked over to help his mom. There wasn't much else he could say. He was pretty sure she was wrong.

He took some of his father's weight and stood on one side.

"Sorry about this, Dad, but we're going to need to walk a bit."

"It's okay..." he muttered. "I've had worse."

They took a few wobbly steps toward the road, and Albert could already feel his back covered in sweat. He wasn't made for this much physical activity, and the world had already battered him. It didn't matter that the strange cold air hadn't gone away and cooled his aching muscles: he was utterly worn out.

As they took a few more steps, he saw Saanvi talking to a pair of what looked to be college students. They were siblings, or at least cousins. The similarities of their light brown hair, deeper brown skin, and brown eyes were too much for them not to be related.

After a brief discussion, both nodded and walked over to Albert. The boy stepped forward and smiled. He scanned his gaze up and down Albert so quickly it was almost impossible to notice.

"Hi there," he said.

"Hi," Albert weakly mumbled.

"Sean."

"Albert."

"You going to be okay to do this?"

"...sure."

Sean nodded. "Yeah ... fair enough. Let me know if you have any trouble balancing."

"Okay."

Sean gave Albert another once-over, then turned away. After just as quickly saying a few pleasantries to his mom, Sean took her place holding up Albert's dad.

Albert took a moment to relax his already aching shoulders. It was a blissful sixty-ish seconds.

"Ready?" Sean eventually called over.

"Yeah."

Sean nodded and walked his dad forward. Albert adjusted and did what he could to help. It really was making it easier having Sean's help. Only a faint puff of exhaustion came out of Albert's mouth every few steps and he didn't fall over.

Once he'd gotten situated into the slightly easier routine, the girl walked beside him.

"Hi there."

"Uh, hi," Albert said.

"I'm Piper. We'll try to help. I can take over when you get too tired."

"Thanks," Albert said. "That's really nice of you and your brother to help."

"Yes, it is. Thanks so much, Piper," Albert's mom agreed, having caught her breath. She walked over to Albert's side and rubbed at her raw-looking eyes.

"You're welcome," Piper replied. "We were in our basement when it happened. I didn't even see it. The world just started shaking. I think it was an earthquake?"

Albert frowned. That wasn't it.

"But the sky…" Albert muttered, casting his gaze on that orange and red tapestry above.

He wasn't the only one doing it, either. As the mass of people migrated to the center of the town, people kept looking at it and muttering.

"Must be something to do with testing," his mother said. "I think the government must have tested something in the atmosphere."

"I don't know why they would test here, though," Piper said.

Albert looked up again and thought of aliens, governmental programs, or whatever could've caused this. He almost didn't notice when, after another step, his legs wobbled, and he practically fell over. An exhausted whine leaked out of him.

"Oh my god, Albert. Let Piper take over," his mom said. "You look like you're going to pass out."

"Okay… thanks."

He looked down at his feet, and it slowly dawned on him how much more he would need to walk.

The walk showed more of the town than Albert had ever seen. First off was the population. Albert had always assumed that once he'd moved away, so had most people his age—but Quill Point was a much younger town than expected.

Teenagers, fellow twenty-somethings, and even young-looking parents spilled onto the path, covered in dust, bruises, or simply looking haggard. They, as he had, were helping escort people injured or otherwise unable to travel the distance easily. Some people were carrying young children or lugging supplies.

He also got to see what the storm, or whatever it was, had done to the town. At least fifteen houses he passed had trees collapsed on them. Fence posts were lying in the street, sometimes still connected to other pieces. Stop signs were tilted, their bases sticking up through the dirt.

It had been a long time since Albert had considered this place his home, but something in his chest was still growing tight.

He stopped examining things too closely when he saw a man crying in front of a house with flowers painted on the front door. Its windows were blasted inward, and a telephone pole had busted a hole in a wall.

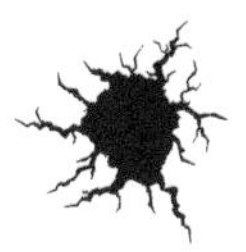

It took until nightfall for Albert to reach the town center. Between his dad's injuries and his aching body, three miles had turned into three hours of walking.

As sunset finished, the moon rose. It crested above the hill that the town center sat on. It looked wrong.

Even though it had only been a half-moon the day before, the moon was full. Its light cast long shadows across the ground, swallowing Albert in the darkness of its glare. Even as his parents walked into the center, he couldn't help but keep standing and staring.

The surface was too smooth: no pockmarks, no craters. An unblemished yellow and white egg was hanging over their heads. A spotlight, a cruel focal point, on this town. The small, tiny, little town of Quill Point.

"Hey, are you coming?"

Albert finally looked down. He hadn't even noticed that he was panting. That his entire body was shaking, vibrating. His heart rate was a horrible thrum in his chest.

Piper was standing there, head tilted slightly. Her eyes bore into his.

"The moon is wrong," he said simply.

She didn't look up, but nodded. She had something on her face that failed to be a smile.

"I know." Her voice was small, barely escaping into the air. "I don't like looking up at it. I don't know what's happening."

"I don't either," Albert said.

She held out her hand. It was shaking.

"Come on, let's go inside… maybe we can figure all this out. Maybe someone knows something."

Albert stared at her hand. His pulse was still racing. It was slightly hard to breathe.

"Do you believe that?"

Piper's mouth became a tight line. She looked like she might cry.

"I'm going to go wait inside, okay? Maybe you should come in, too. In case your dad needs help."

Before he could say anything more, maybe even apologize, she turned around and walked into the building. It felt like she was running away, but not from him—not from anything that could be run from.

Albert took one last look at the moon and went inside.

Chapter Three

ALBERT WALKED INTO A HIGH-CEILINGED room full of murmurs and nervous faces. He found his parents in the right corner and walked over, crossing little clusters of people. He spied teenagers huddled together, one passing something between them—a small silver flask. A trio of children ran in circles, laughing.

At the far end of the room, toward a dais, stood about ten people in police uniforms. They seemed to be discussing something important. A few waved their hands, passionate about whatever they were saying.

Albert's parents were, by contrast, rather taciturn. His mom had a distant gaze, wringing her hands repeatedly. His father was sitting on a bench, barely awake. Occasionally, he'd rub at the sore spot on his head where the bookcase had hit him.

"What do we do now?" Albert asked.

"The mayor is apparently on his way," his mother said. "He'll address the town and tell us the plan."

Albert nodded. It didn't feel like a good enough answer. The sky had changed—surely the military or the government would show up with white suits and massive trucks and take charge. That was how it always worked in the movies.

Or were they busy handling things in major cities? How widespread *was* this? Did the phones and cars not work across all of America? What about airplanes? Was this happening to the whole planet?

His hands tightened at his side. His thoughts kept getting louder.

"What about a doctor?" Albert eventually asked.

"No one's … heard from them," his dad replied. "I'm feeling… I'm feeling a lot better now. I guess all that … fresh air did me good."

He let out the weakest and fakest laugh Albert had ever heard.

Albert swallowed hard. He was sure he was about to cry. "I'll go … see if anyone is saying anything."

He wandered off, unable to look at his parent suffering like this. He wanted to scream or yell for help—but *everyone* needed help. His dad wasn't the only one injured. Ten people, *at least,* had broken bones. Someone mentioned a nasty concussion during the walk.

The only distraction was the building itself.

The best way to describe the building was as a repurposed church. There was no stained glass or Bibles, but the seating was mostly lines of pews looking upon a dais with a shiny wood lectern, and the ceiling vaulted up into almost darkness.

This single room alone was enormous, easily holding a hundred or more people. The door he'd entered had gone straight here, but he could see other doorways to presumably more rooms. For a small town, it had a sizeable governmental budget.

As he wandered, he came upon a framed picture. It had its own section of wall. Small twin lights on either side made sure it didn't get swallowed up in the inadequately lit space.

It was of an older woman. Her hair was silvery, and her face was pale white and wrinkled. She had heterochromia and a sharp gaze.

"Irena Ink," he mumbled.

Everyone who had ever lived in Quill Point learned of the founder. And it was hard to forget her with the town's aggressive naming convention. But it had been so long since he'd seen a picture.

As he looked at it closely, the face seemed to … shift. Not quite move. Just wobble or pixelate. The mouth was especially fuzzy and hard to look at. Albert rubbed his eyes. The tiredness that had never left got aggressive again. It was amazing he could focus his eyes on anything.

Albert sat in one of the pews. It wasn't comfortable. The cushion was worn and lacking in padding. His body told him to sleep—his mind refused the notion. He sat there and breathed for a moment. His eyes drifted closed as his mind buzzed, whirred, and spat out formless worries.

After a few moments of slowly calming himself down, he heard a shuffle. When Albert opened his eyes and turned his head, he found a little boy smiling. The kid had black hair, brown eyes, white skin, and was missing a tooth in the middle of his smile. He couldn't be older than ten.

"Hi!" the boy said.

Albert tried to smile. "Hi."

"What's your name?" the boy asked.

"Albert. What's yours?"

The boy tilted his head and giggled. "I was trying not to have one."

"You were trying not to have one?" Albert echoed.

"Yep."

"Okay…" Albert said. "Where are your parents?"

"Nearby. He's not scared like you."

Albert ran his hand through his hair. That was the thing about kids. Kids have no filter. He wasn't sure he wanted to continue this line of conversation. He wasn't sure *he* could handle it.

"You can tell I'm scared?" Albert asked.

"People are afraid of the sky. They're really scared."

"And you're not?"

The boy smiled. If Albert didn't know better, he would've said the look was mischievous, a little taunting.

"Why is the sky changing color scary?" the boy asked. "It changes colors every day."

"This is different. Did the boom not scare you?"

"I like thunder. Scary things are a lot of fun. I like what's happening with the sky."

Albert looked off to the side. Was it his responsibility to correct a kid about this? Albert didn't like knowing how bad it all was. If he didn't know that the sky was alien, the moon staring, and the world possibly ending, would *he* want to know?

But all the lies felt bitter on his tongue before he even spoke them.

"It wasn't … thunder. That's not what thunder sounds like. Something bad is happening. You should be careful."

"What about it is bad?" the boy asked and then giggled. "It's fun, isn't it? I like this new sky. It feels better than the old sky."

"People aren't happy about the sky."

The boy cocked his head. "That doesn't matter. Why would what people think matter?"

Albert stared at this kid. "Where did you say your parents were again?"

He smiled, the gap interrupting rows of teeth. "Nearby, around, present—like they say at roll call. 'Present' or 'here,' everyone says. That's what kids say. That's what all the kids say."

Albert flinched. He couldn't tell why that sounded weird.

"Are you playing a game?" Albert asked.

"Not yet."

Albert blinked a few times. He wasn't sure if he'd messed up the conversation, said something wrong, or if the kid was teasing him.

"Maybe you should go see your parents," Albert said. "Give them a hug."

"But I'm talking to you."

"Yes, but I bet your parents are worried. They could use a hug with how scary the thunder is. Besides, you shouldn't really be talking to strangers."

"Okay, Albert. I'll not talk to you anymore. You don't like the sky. Where are *your* parents, then?"

Albert turned his head to point them out, but the kid was already wandering off when he turned back. The kid didn't glance back at him and sat down with three other boys around some board game.

Albert frowned. It was an innocent enough sight, and yet something felt off. He didn't have time to consider it further; a murmur spread throughout the room.

A clean-shaven and imposingly tall man in a blue and expensive-looking suit was moving through the crowd as if he owned it. They kept parting for him until he reached the dais and stood behind the lectern. The police officers made a ring around the spot. Several people drifted to pews and sat down.

The crackle of a mic going live echoed through the room. A sharp blast of feedback burst out, and the sound system faded to a faint hiss.

"Hello, Quill Point citizens," the man said, his voice calm and slow. "Thank you for coming here and being so organized. We are currently working on figuring out what has happened. We don't yet know what caused the sudden boom we all experienced. Nor do we have any answers about what has been happening with cell phones and vehicles. All other electronics have shown themselves to work, and if this is not handled by today, everyone should have working heat in their homes—"

"I have a question!"

A hand was up, waving back and forth. The crowd parted around the person, drifting back like they were putting off a force field.

She was short and had pale white skin. She wore a tie-dyed shirt and jeans covered in what looked like flecks of clay. Her hair was almost as colorful as her shirt, with purple, pink, and red streaks almost completely drowning out her auburn hair.

She hopped once, then shook her hand again. "Come on! I have a question!"

The man stared at her, a slight frown on his lips. "I hardly think this is the time—"

"You have to answer! It's in the bylaws. Which *you* wrote!"

"Okay ... what is your question?"

"What about those of us whose houses got wrecked?!"

The man nodded at that, his frown turning into a tight smile. He took a deep breath—audible through the mic—then gathered himself again.

"Thank you for asking, Brianna—"

"Bree," she loudly corrected.

"Yes, thank you for asking, *Bree*. The Kraken Hotel has agreed to supply lodging for anyone whose shelter was destroyed by this event. We'll be rounding everyone up interested in that after this meeting. Now, I would please ask anyone else with questions—"

This time, Albert's mother's hand was up.

"Is there anyone coming with medical experience? My husband is hurt."

"Unfortunately," the man said, "we've needed every licensed practitioner at the hospital to help the patients there. Several people are in critical condition because of this event. If it's an emergency, one of the officers can escort you. But, if it's minor, it would help greatly if you just grin and bear it. We don't have the usual support of the surrounding towns' services and have limited police and medical personnel at our disposal."

Albert's mother's hand dropped, and she sat beside her husband. She looked deflated. Her gaze was downcast. Albert quietly walked to the back end of the pews and made his way over to them. His father gave him a nod when he sat down.

"I truly am sorry," the mayor said, then cleared his throat. "Now, I wanted to ask for a few volunteers. We need some groups to make an expedition out of the town. As I said, we've gotten no indication of any aid coming in. I've already sent every available officer we can spare, but it won't be enough. The sooner we can contact the greater government, the sooner we can get this awful day behind us. So, I ask, who's willing to go?"

Murmurs passed through the crowd, spiking in places, but no one called out to volunteer. The mayor surveyed the crowd, looking pointedly at a few people. After slightly rolling his eyes, he moved to talk into the microphone again.

"I've spoken with the authorities. I've spoken with the firefighters. We do *not* have the manpower. To keep order, we need some of them here to ensure the safety of the citizenry of Quill Point. I've had officers discuss this. They've told me that groups of five people would be best."

"I'll do it."

A tall, thin guy with a thick, curling mustache and deeply tanned white skin stood up from a pew and made his way to the front.

The mayor nodded. "Thank you. That's one so far. I need to stress this here, citizens of Quill Point: If we want things to go back to normal, we need people to go out and tell someone what's happening to this town. It's an act of charity!"

"Why can't you go!?" Bree yelled.

The mayor fixed her with a glare. "Because I need to be here to oversee things until we can get to some kind of normalcy, dear. This town will need some degree of overseeing if it's going to handle this crisis with the poise and tact expected of us."

"Fine," she said. "Then why don't you pick some people to go if you want to lead us so much?"

As Albert kept looking at the two, he noticed they had the same small nose and arch to their jaw. The rich kids hadn't attended the same high school he had, but he'd heard the mayor had a daughter. He wondered...

"If no one will step forward," the mayor said, "then I shall be forced to make a more direct request of a few citizens to do their civic duty. But I would rather have a few people go of their own accord."

"Fine, I'm on it," called a voice a few feet from Albert.

Albert turned to see a guy step off from leaning against a wall. He had dark brown skin and wore a large shirt with a superhero on it. He apparently knew the first guy because he nodded as he approached.

"Thank you, as well," the mayor said. "Is anyone else willing to go for the good of everyone here?"

"I'll do it," came another voice. This one was feminine. A woman in perhaps her late twenties, with wispy blond hair and a pink complexion, stepped forward. "I was probably going to go by myself, anyway."

"Thank you so much as well. I appreciate the cooperation. We do need to speed things along. It's already dark out. I, for one, do not want slow decision-making to interfere with what needs to be *done*."

The idea slid into Albert's head: *he* could go. If it weren't for his car, he wouldn't still be in town. They needed volunteers. He was exhausted and sore, but it wasn't like he would get any sleep. A thrum of anxiety was so deep in his blood that he would just stare at the ceiling for hours.

He looked at his parents. Wouldn't this be the best way to help them?

He barely noticed that he'd already raised his hand.

"Thank you, sir. I'm glad we can move this along. I don't recognize you, though."

Several eyes snapped on him. Albert flinched but still stood up. His mom stared at him with wide eyes.

"Uh, I'm Albert, Albert Turner," he said, gesturing at his father. "My parents are—"

"Oh, you're the Turners' son. Well, glad to see some help from even the extended Quill Point family. Come up here, and we can get this expedition going. We just need one more person to begin."

Albert walked slowly. Even after just today, he recognized so many faces in the crowd. Henry and his wife, Saanvi. Sean and Piper. Bree. Cynthia and the tall woman with brown skin he assumed was her wife.

And the little boy, who smiled mischievously at him with his missing tooth.

As he walked, the blood rushed to his head. He was going back out there with the sky and the moon. He swallowed a buildup of spit, and his mouth felt too dry.

As he waited with the group, his mom still staring at him, trying to communicate something without words, a fifth person walked over.

She wore a floral dress and had tanned, white skin. Her hair had small paper butterflies in it. Around her neck was a small charm, a closed pendant with a cross etched in the metal.

Albert vaguely recognized her. It took a long moment for him to place the memory. He'd been a kid the last time he'd seen that face.

"Ms. Daffodil?" he whispered.

She nodded and smiled. Now he remembered. He remembered her classroom, his preschool classroom, and all the namesake flowers people would bring her on her birthday.

"You've grown up, Albert," she said. "Nice to see you back."

The overpowering smell of flowers hit him. She'd always done that, wearing the same scent for decades. He wondered if she liked the branding, the story she'd made for herself.

"Are you sure you want to make a trip like this?" he asked.

She smirked. It was something he couldn't ever recall her doing before. All he could remember was a sweet demeanor and lots of teaching phonics.

"Oh, I've been hiking before. Much further than this. A straight line to the next town over is better than dealing with this chaos. It makes preschool seem like a cakewalk."

She cast out her hand as people awkwardly formed lines, and multiple discussions happened—some rather loudly—over the finer points of migrating tens of people into a hotel without giving them a chance to go back and get clothing. Albert could distinctly hear Bree arguing with who Albert was now suspecting was her father.

"I'd prefer sugar-high kids over the politicians," Ms. Daffodil said.

Albert couldn't help but chuckle. It felt good and made him feel guilty to laugh while all this was happening.

"Okay… that's good," Albert said.

"Nothing to worry about. I'll be fine." She smiled again. "It's so nice to see you, Al. Nice to know you grew up such a good kid."

"I wouldn't say that." Albert looked down at his feet for a second. "But thank you."

"Oh, you're a good kid. I can see it."

"…thanks."

Albert was looking anywhere else when he spied his mom making her way over to him. She still had a hardened look on her face. He wasn't sure he understood it—but it didn't seem happy. His dad followed. He could walk on his own now, but moved off-balance and kept wincing.

"Hello, Gretchen," his mother said to Ms. Daffodil.

Even after all these years, it felt odd to Albert to hear anyone refer to his teacher by anything but her last name.

"Hello there, Georgina," she replied. "I was just saying hi to your son. It's been a long time."

"Yeah, it has been a while," she said, then fixed her gaze on Albert.

"Ah," Ms. Daffodil said. "I'll give you some space. Albert and I will have plenty of time to talk during our little walk."

"Thanks," Georgina said.

Ms. Daffodil gave a sympathetic smile and meandered over to the other four people about to make the trip. They made a clean little circle. Albert frowned.

His mom talked around a deep frown. "What do you think you're doing?"

"I'm helping them out," Albert said, absentmindedly fiddling with his hands. "You heard the mayor. He said he needed people to go find out what's happening. I want to help."

"Your father got hit by a bookcase! Let someone else go do it."

Albert looked at his dad. "Are you okay?"

His dad winced and rubbed at the spot, but nodded. "I am. But I still don't feel like you should go out there. Whatever happens, we'd rather you be close by."

Albert struggled to think of what to say. He'd been moved out for so long—it had been such a long time since his parents had given him anything close to a command.

"I..." he began, then sighed. "I really do want to go with them. I want to. Whatever this is, it's way bigger than we think it is. If the world... if it's happening everywhere, I *need* to help."

"It could be really dangerous, Albert," his mom said.

Albert couldn't look at her pleading eyes, the sadness and anger and something else in them.

"I think it's dangerous everywhere right now. I feel like if I don't do something about it, and something *does* happen, I'm going to feel sick with myself."

"It's not your responsibility," his mom said.

Albert couldn't help but feel a spark of anger. He'd worked at a startup because making software could tangibly help people—but it mostly became placating shareholders.

"No, it's not my responsibility. But I'm part of the problem if I think like that."

As quickly as it had hit him, the anger deflated. He felt even more tired—a tired that went well past his bones, down to the core of himself. He delivered his following words with a voice flat and exhausted.

"I feel like I have to try something. It's just a trip, Mom. It's going to be fine."

His mom might have said something more, but his dad put a hand on her arm. Something passed between them. Albert wished he could know what it was.

"Okay," his mom said, hesitancy dripping from each syllable. "If you really have to. But please be careful. If something really bad is happening, make sure *you're* okay."

Albert opened and then closed his mouth. If he said anything more, he might change his mind—or someone would cry. He just hugged his mom.

When his parents left, his mom turned away a little too fast. Probably so he wouldn't see her cry.

It was eerily like when he'd left for Silicon Valley—like the first night he'd spent in his apartment—a life shift with an organic, inevitable, and ruthless finality.

Chapter Four

ALBERT LEARNED MORE NAMES IN ONE day than he had in the first month of work. And what made it all the more surprising was that, for each one he learned, he was increasingly aware of the people he hadn't even *seen*. The small town was more a web of interlocking personalities than a municipality. The four people he was walking with were more vibrantly themselves than he'd ever felt.

He got to know Chuck and Patrick.

Chuck was the one with a superhero on his shirt. He talked quickly and owned the only comic book shop in Quill Point. Albert knew plenty of people who worked in tech with similar introverted but overwhelmingly friendly personalities. He offered everyone gum, but only Patrick took it.

Patrick's handlebar mustache was even more impressive up close. On his left arm was a finished tattoo sleeve and, on his right, a half-finished one. He talked even faster than Chuck—it reminded Albert of an auctioneer.

He apparently volunteered because he had a better plan than walking toward the nearest town. They stood near the town center's front door and discussed it as the mayor continued to ask for more five-person groups in the background.

"So, my uncle, a big member of the Quill Point survivalists, has this place at the edge of town, and he's agreed for it to be a bit of a waystation. He's going to stay at the hotel. His knee's not at all, even a little, great. It's maybe two miles, at the most, and then we can stay there—get up early—and then we can get this done. Is everyone okay with that?"

"You know I'm on board," Chuck said. "It's a better place than you'd think. Been a while since we've been there."

"Not since that tournament, right?"

"Sounds about right."

"How many rooms does it have?" asked Cassandra.

Cassandra was the woman with wispy hair. She kept looking at her phone like she was going to cry. When she wasn't doing that, she was touching a worn-out friendship bracelet partially hidden under her jacket sleeve.

"It's got two," Patrick replied. "I figured two people could share a room at a time, and there's also a couch."

Albert looked between them all. He wanted to contribute something to this.

"I can take the couch."

"That works for me," Cassandra said. "You okay to share a room, Ms. Daffodil?"

"Yes, that's fine," she said.

"Okay, let's get going then, shall we?" Patrick said. "We're burning moonlight."

Albert hung back slightly as they walked outside and into that moonlight. His feet grew heavier. Each step took an effort to unstick from the ground.

"You always did do that," Ms. Daffodil said, moving next to him.

"I did?" Albert asked, embarrassed.

"Yeah, you always did. You were a shy kid. You'd always be the last person out of the bus when we went on field trips."

Albert managed to smile. "I guess some stuff never changes."

"Maybe," she said and held out her hand. "We can see, I suppose. Would this help?"

He looked at her hand and felt even more embarrassed. But simultaneously, it *would* help.

"I can say that *I* needed it," Ms. Daffodil continued. "People just let you do stuff when you're the sweet old lady they remember from childhood. People remember you more often than they *see* you."

Albert looked at her then. Tried to *see* her. She was an older woman with flowers and warmth. That much was easy. He took her hand and held it. Her grip was firmer than he'd expected.

He looked down at her hand and saw a scar—a jagged white line traced from her thumb's knuckle down to her wrist.

She noticed and chuckled. "I tell people it was an accident with some craft scissors."

"I'm guessing it wasn't?"

"Nope. As I said, people see you as an old lady. And that I had a large purse."

"Oh."

"Don't worry, he's fine."

That got an unexpected chuckle out of Albert. More an act of surprise than finding it funny.

"Um, okay."

"You're safe with me," Ms. Daffodil said. "But we should go."

They walked into that unseasonably cold breeze. Rather than look up at the horrible moon, Albert kept his gaze focused on her hand. The darkness outside was sudden and intense, much worse than it had been earlier; he could barely see her individual fingers.

"It was a knife, then?" he asked. It was an unneeded question, but it was also a distracting question.

She didn't answer at first. She'd looked up. The entire group had done the same. Stared up.

Albert didn't want to know.

But still, he looked.

There was *nothing*. Over the past few nights, he'd been reminded of how many stars he could see in this tiny town, how they speckled the entire dome of sight with angel-light pinpricks. But now they were simply gone. Only the moon, that featureless moon, was in the sky.

Albert felt like it was pressing down on him. Like the sky would crush him into the same dark nothingness that had consumed the stars.

"It was a knife, yeah," Ms. Daffodil eventually said.

Her voice was so tiny that Albert was almost unsure he'd heard it. But he didn't ask her to repeat it. He looked and looked, and then someone said something about moving—maybe Chuck, maybe Cassandra—and he stopped looking. It was like airplane ear finally passing.

No one said anything else. They just started walking.

The streets were wide open and dark, with each streetlight a single orange beacon, insufficient in every regard. The faint wind made the trees and plant life into a shifting mass. More than once, Albert could swear he saw someone standing, waving to him out in the dark, only for it to be a fern or small bush rustling in the wind.

It would be a long couple of miles.

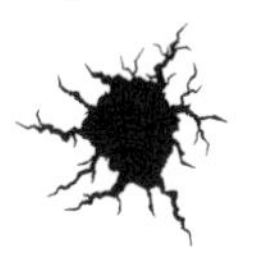

"Almost there," Chuck called out from somewhere in front.

Albert had been waiting to hear that for so long that he'd almost given up on it—like they would wander the streets forever, mocked by the moon and swallowed by the dark.

"About time," Cassandra said. "I was on my feet the whole day today."

Albert barely spied their destination. It was a squarish dark lump fringed by many trees. The trees seemed to reach out for the building, their thin branches latticing on the triangular roof.

"Here we are," Chuck said.

"It's honestly kind of small. The top floor is really just an attic," Patrick chimed in. "But we'll only need to stay for one night, so it should work."

"Does it have anything to drink?" Cassandra asked.

"There's water," Patrick replied.

"Not what I meant."

Patrick nodded. "I think my uncle kept a few things. He made his own beer once or twice. I'm sure he has something. Come to think of it, I might want to join you on that. Does anyone else—and not judging, by the way—want something?"

Ms. Daffodil shook her head. "I appreciate the offer, but I've not touched the stuff in a long time."

"Sure," Chuck said. He turned to Albert. "You?"

"I'm good, thanks. I just want to settle."

Chuck nodded, and he, Patrick, and Cassandra went into the building. Light leaked out from several windows, slightly blocked by tree trunks.

"How are you doing?" Ms. Daffodil asked.

Albert swallowed hard. "It's just been a lot. I need to sleep. I wasn't even planning on being here when this started, and now it feels like the whole world has changed on me. It changed so fast … how did it end up like this?"

"You get used to that," she replied. "It's a little like getting older."

That caught Albert off guard. So far, during this walk, his teacher had shown little sign of her age. She had a quick stride and wasn't breathing as heavily as Albert. But with the glow of the window behind her and the darkness everywhere else, she seemed much older than any person ever would be. Her eyes had something tired, weary, and worn.

"Are you okay?" Albert asked.

The look passed, and she smiled. "I'm just worried too, you know. I've taught a lot of kids in my day, Albert, and I worry about all of them. You know that girl with all the clay on her, the one from the meeting?"

"Uh, Bree, right? She's the mayor's daughter, right?"

"Yeah, her. I babysat her before she went off to private school. I've basically known her all her life. I can't imagine anything bad happening to her, to you, to any of my kids."

Her gaze was on him, but it didn't seem like she was seeing him as he was now. Great chunks of childhood were hazy to Albert, long faded. It amazed him someone had parts of his history lost to even himself.

"When I heard you moved away, I was worried about you too," Ms. Daffodil said. "I really am glad to see you turned out well."

"Thanks," was all he could think to respond. He cleared his throat. "I guess we should go meet up with the others."

Ms. Daffodil nodded and moved for the door. Albert was about to do the same when the wind shifted. It shifted *up*. His shirt hem slightly flared.

With the shift came deep anxiety. His hands tightened at his sides. The sensation invaded his senses, pouring down his spine. It was like static electricity was coating his skin.

"*Thirteen.*"

Albert froze, his pulse skyrocketing. He could barely catch his breath.

The voice was clear, enunciated perfectly, and inhuman. A sensation deep in the pit of Albert's stomach spasmed. A primal rush went through his mind.

"*Thirteen.*"

He almost screamed but choked it back. The breeze stopped—the world was too quiet. Ms. Daffodil was only a few feet away, frozen as well.

"What the *fuck*?" he whispered.

His gaze locked onto Ms. Daffodil's back, and he sprinted to her. She jolted when he touched her shoulder, her eyes as wide as he assumed his were.

"It's nearby," Albert whispered.

They bolted for the door and swung it open with a too-loud bang.

The others were still, having clearly heard the noise. Chuck was sitting stiffly on the couch, holding a beer. Cassandra was off in a corner with her own bottle. Patrick stood by a window, one hand resting on an unlit pinball machine.

He started to say something.

Ms. Daffodil shushed him.

Patrick stiffened, then mouthed: *What was that?*

Ms. Daffodil looked over at Albert. Before he could make any motion, the sound came again. Closer. Louder. With almost a mocking tone.

"*Thirteen.*"

Cassandra let out a single shriek before covering her mouth.

Albert swallowed hard and looked frantically at each window. Four were around the room—all the curtains drawn back. All of them looked like a pit, nothing but shadows and shifting branches.

"Do you have a gun?" Ms. Daffodil whispered.

Patrick's eyes went wide. He pursed his lips and slowly shook his head.

That anxious sensation came again and hit like a truck, almost knocking Albert to the ground. His eyes twitched from the surge.

"*Thirteen!*"

Everyone jolted. It was right outside. A slow scrabbling above. It was the sound of claws on the roof slates; there was no mistaking it for anything else.

Cassandra clutched her stomach against a stifled scream.

Chuck went into the kitchen, getting a chef's knife from its wooden block. He held it with shaking hands. Ms. Daffodil quickly joined him and pulled free a paring knife.

Patrick was at the window, tilting his head, looking up. Trying to catch a glimpse of someone on the roof.

A rumble started far away but was building—vibrating the air and rolling toward them. The thunder that wasn't thunder. The sound that started this nightmarish new reality.

Only now, it was a voice.

"*THIRTEEN!*"

A crash of glass. The window next to Patrick exploded into shards and rushing wind. A massive claw of viscous dark engulfed his face, covering his eyes and mouth, and yanked him away. A pop of blood trailed behind, splattering across the couch.

Patrick's single scream echoed into the night.

Albert's body felt encased in stone, holding down his voice, his lungs, his muscles. Nobody was moving. Everyone was holding their breath.

The voice was definitely mocking.

"*Twelve.*"

Chapter Five

EVERYONE SCRAMBLED AWAY FROM THE windows and doors. They stood in a cluster in the middle of the room. Albert glanced at each potential entry point, scrutinizing the darkness to see if that hand was reaching in.

The sound on the roof stopped. A single moment of peace before a new noise started. A slow scratching sound. It was coming from nearby, but it was hard to place exactly where. It got increasingly rhythmic.

Ms. Daffodil's arm shot up, pointing at a spot on the wall. The plaster, followed by wood shavings, was flaking out from a small hole. The dust floated down in a tiny snowstorm.

It wasn't the only hole for long.

The entire room was being drilled into, pried at, eaten. The walls became a hive, burrowed into faster than any ant could ever manage.

Albert felt pressure brush his shoe. He looked down to find wooden shavings pushed up around a hole in the rug. It wasn't like any bug he'd ever seen. It was a single, worming tendril the color of night. Thick, acrid smoke floated off it like it was burning.

"*Twelve.*"

Something snapped in Albert. Anxiety overcame everything. He bolted. He flung open the door and ran into the night. A horrific crack sounded behind him. Then a sharp series of pops. Then gunshot-loud cracks.

People were screaming. He didn't know which ones. Someone was running behind him. The wind was shifting upward again. It was too much. It was too loud. It was too *much*.

Pieces of wood flew over his head. Entire boards rained from the sky. Half of the front door skidded across the pavement.

He ran even faster. His lungs seized in his chest, choking him, but he still ran faster. He would've been screaming, but he didn't have enough air to do both.

The other runner got close; it was Ms. Daffodil in his periphery. They barely acknowledged each other as they sprinted away from the house, from something that could *destroy* an entire house.

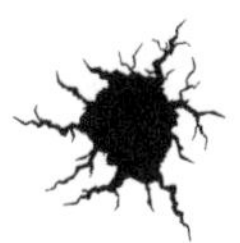

After almost half a mile, it became obvious nothing was chasing them. It was silent again. The booming voice hadn't announced any other numbers.

Albert slowed, then stopped. He was gasping. He wanted to puke, but nothing came out of his throat. It occurred to him only now that he'd had nothing to eat or drink since the coffee a lifetime ago. An aching hunger twisted in his gut. A surge of lightheadedness almost plunged him to the ground.

Ms. Daffodil stopped next to him, the knife still clutched at her side.

"Where did they—" Albert gasped out, then wheezed. He put his hands on his knees and sucked in air. He was almost glad it had gotten colder since the sky had changed.

"They went out the back of the house, into the woods," Ms. Daffodil said. Even she sounded out of breath. "I don't know if they're okay."

"What ... was ... *that*?" Albert asked.

Ms. Daffodil's hand tightened on the knife. "I don't know... I don't know."

Albert straightened up, still panting. He looked back, but he couldn't see the remains of the house. The dark swallowed it at this distance.

"We need to get back to the center," Albert said. "Warn someone..."

"But what about them?"

Albert took a deep breath. "I don't even think they're..."

He stopped talking. His old preschool teacher was crying. An adult that was an adult the entire time he'd been alive was *crying*. He'd seen his mom and dad cry—but this was different. If someone like her was afraid...

This was wrong, like everything else. Like the sky, like the monstrous hand. This was *fucking* wrong.

Albert put his hand over his mouth, and tears came quickly.

Patrick was dead. Chuck and Cassandra were probably dead. Anyone else could be. Monsters, aliens, demons, or something else were real. The world might be ending, now, today, in the dark.

And he didn't even know where his *parents* were. He'd fucking left them. His mother, who made the worst days better. His father, who taught him to care for others even above himself. They could be dead for all he knew. Another number.

Why had he been in such a hurry to leave?

"*Twelve!*"

Albert screamed so deep his voice cracked. He clutched his head.

"*Eleven!*"

Ms. Daffodil let out her own scream, and Albert's head snapped up. Something was stretching down in front of them, lowering itself.

Albert's mind failed to parse it. To accept what he was seeing. It was like a movie effect, a computer-made impossibility. Nothing in the real world looked like that.

It was a column. A wide and thick column of darkness leaking black smoke. It stretched down from the sky. When it touched the ground, it expanded outward. From its center mass came tendrils and massive clawed hands.

With the crack of a whip, a hand shot out into the darkness, then went taut. A single vibration went down the length of it. It pulled back fast.

The hand dragged a man by his nose, the claw's tip bursting through the top of his head. His shoes scuffed across the pavement.

As quickly as it was there, it tossed the corpse into a sudden and mouth-shaped hole in the darkness, then pulled back upward. It was a pure dark elevator, disappearing into that endless place with no stars.

He watched the man go. As he did, his eyes widened. A spasm went through his chest, his throat. Albert tried to form any other thought, to think past the expanding realization, but it wouldn't stop. It was all that could fit in his mind.

He tilted back his head.

It was not a starless sky.

"It's above us…" he whispered.

It blotted out the *whole sky*.

A muscular rumble shifted across that satin flesh, that impossibly enormous creature that sat above them, somehow not crushing them, somehow blanketing the whole of what Albert could see.

It shifted, and Albert realized in some small part of his mind that it was *breathing in for another rumbling cry.*

"*Ten,*" the beast above shouted.

Albert fell. He couldn't stand up anymore. More columns descended. They were darker than the night. Voids in contrast. They keened and screeched as they dropped. Albert smelled something meaty and foul that grew so strong he vomited bile.

Ms. Daffodil was still screaming. He might've been too. He couldn't quite hear himself.

A column slapped down a hundred feet away. As it writhed and grew limbs, a claw burst from the earth. Rocks and dirt scattered as the claw unfolded itself.

It wobbled in the air. Newborn. Sensing. Looking at Albert.

Ms. Daffodil ran past him, holding the knife above her head. She charged directly at it.

A pulse ran through the ground—a building vibration. Then the hand snapped out like a cobra, fingers spread and sharp.

Albert reached out to Ms. Daffodil, yelling her name.

The hand hit her on the shoulder. She stumbled from the force; the knife flew out of her hand. The claw turned. A finger lanced into the side of her neck, pointing upward—sliding upward.

She went limp instantly.

Her eyes dropped, rolling like marbles toward gravity's whims.

The force of the hand snapping back, pulling her toward the column, was like she'd been thrown sideways. The hole opened, dragged her inside, and took her from sight.

Albert cried and screamed at the column as it stole her away. He kicked and flailed backward, unable to stand, howling at the heavens. His entire body shook—like he was sobbing with every muscle.

"*Nine!*"

More columns descended. They were doubling, tripling in numbers. They crashed down like meteor strikes—like giant feet pounding the earth as they scooped away life.

"*Eight!*"

Albert expected to die.

"*Seven!*"

It would take him. There was no escaping the sky, no running from something like this.

"*Six!*"

He could hear screams in the dark. Groups yelling and shouting and howling. Pistol and rifle fire echoed out. How many people had been outside?

"*Five!*"

The wind got colder. Albert's hands grew numb. The tears still streaming down his face hurt. He couldn't stop staring at the impossibly large mass that blotted out the stars.

"*Four!*"

The world was going to end.

This was it.

No helping people. No saving anyone. No life. No future. No future girlfriend. No more family.

All of it was gone.

"*Three!*"

He was tiny. It was so much larger than him. It hurt his mind to conceive of the edges—of what could be that large. How could it exist at all?

"*Two!*"

The columns dropped in clusters. They pounded the earth and shook the ground. Sections of trees flattened. Houses burst. The keening sound grew into a shrill laugh. Even though it was far away, it echoed in Albert's head.

"*One!*"

The hands didn't need columns anymore. They were larger than columns. The sky shifted and writhed as two hands dipped through the dark layer, each larger than buildings. Their motions moved the treetops with a wind like a hurricane's.

They curled down, converging on one spot. Albert whimpered. Somewhere in town, they slammed together with an ear-splitting boom, then lifted something into the sky.

"*None!*"

The wind howled. The sky flashed with glimpses of a million twisting hands coiling and writhing. The air itself thrummed.

Albert expected *everyone* to die.

The moon faded around the edges. It grew smaller. A shrinking aperture. It snapped shut, and every light in the town was extinguished. It was dark—it was endless and dark.

And still, Albert was alive.

Cold and alive.

Albert could only hear his crying. He couldn't see. He didn't notice when all the adrenaline faded; he lost consciousness, slumping against the ground.

Chapter Six

ALBERT DREAMED NIGHTMARES SO VILE he got not one bit of real rest. He awoke to daylight. Someone was calling out names. Different names. It made his head pound.

All of him hurt. His body was sore in ways he couldn't put into exact words. It was like the merest hint of preparing a muscle to move was enough to send shooting agony. He clutched his head and forced open a single eye.

The sky was still that horrible red and orange. Its streaks moved out from the far-away storm clouds. But the dark mass was gone.

Or waiting.

He sat up and let out a whimpering groan. The muscles in his stomach stabbed at him. He barely held himself up before slumping forward, his hands wrapped around his middle.

"Albert? Albert!"

Albert lifted his head slowly. A group of people was walking toward him. They were a blurry collection of colors and outlines. One was coming toward him faster than the others.

"Albert, you're okay!"

"Mom?" he croaked, his throat hating the act of speaking.

He nearly screamed when she hugged him. The embrace hurt so much. But he didn't let it stop. He leaned into it, somehow still finding more water to cry.

"I was…" his mother tried to say, but her sobbing caught the words. "I was *so* worried about you."

A moment later, another pair of arms wrapped around him.

"Thank god," his father said. "Thank god you're okay."

"I'm sorry…" Albert managed.

"It's okay. It's all okay," his mother instantly replied.

But Albert felt like he had to say it. He had to make the words come out through the pain. He owed them that, at the very least.

"I'm sorry I didn't stay."

"It's okay, son," his father replied. "We know you just wanted to… we're just glad you're okay."

"It was… the sky was…"

"We know," his mother said, her voice growing quieter.

"I was so scared," Albert said. He shuddered and kept shuddering. Whenever he felt like he could stop, the images of the sky would reenter his head, and he would fall apart again.

He didn't know how long the moment lasted. How long his parents held him as his mind replayed hell. If they said anything else to him, he didn't hear it.

It could've been hours. But eventually, they had to move. Albert's lips were cracked, and his stomach was raging. There was water and food back at the town center.

His parents helped him walk.

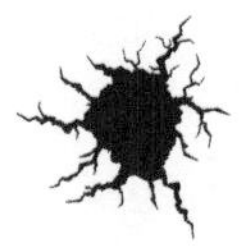

Albert had a question he didn't want to ask; he wasn't sure he could handle the answer. But as they walked through a damaged Quill Point, full of obliterated homes, flattened craters, and an unearthly sky, the question became bigger and bigger in his mind.

"Who else… who else was taken?"

Albert wasn't sure there was a worse answer than no one answering. The silence was a stab in the heart. Ms. Daffodil had such a distinct scream—he could hear it in his head with little effort.

"Was… was it only thirteen?!" he pressed. "Did only thirteen people die out there?"

His mother eventually answered, "We don't know."

Albert deflated. Of course, they didn't know. How could anyone know? The people around him could be some of the only people left on the planet.

"Okay…" Albert said.

The group fell silent again. There was a while left to walk.

Albert noticed the others tensing before he saw it. Murmurs spread. His father's face grew pale, and he wouldn't look forward.

And some part of Albert's mind knew that he shouldn't either. That in this new world, looking was dangerous in itself. But the impulse was so fast, so full of burning curiosity, he didn't have time to stop himself.

He instantly wished he hadn't looked.

It touched the sky. A dark spire. The surrounding air was fuzzy, like an optical illusion not yet in focus. The red and orange tendrils of the sky turned solid and wrapped down its length.

Being by it was like gravity. The ground may have been flat and level, but Albert was at the lip of a bowl, a sharp incline, the spire at the center. He *had* to go toward it. There was no other choice.

He didn't realize he was already in motion—that he was gaining speed. His mother's hand glanced off his arm. No one could stop this impulse.

"Albert!" someone yelled.

But he didn't listen.

The spire was made of gray, pockmarked stone. On its surface, half-formed and unfinished symbols sparked with red light. Those symbols warped the air. They coated the area in a staticky fog.

Albert wasn't the only one pulled into the spire's orbit. Many people had already arrived, forming a loose circle. Some cried. Some sang wordless songs. Others simply stood still, enraptured.

Only when he had passed the throng could he see the bodies. The corpses. The thirteen people the sky had claimed for itself.

They formed a circle, facing outward from the spire.

Each had their knees beneath them, and their hands held rigidly toward the sky. It almost looked like prayer songs with their heads tilted back, mouths agape.

But they were not singing.

Deep rot consumed their tongues, teeth, and mouths' inner flesh. The top part of their heads was gone. The eyes, forehead, and hair were removed like the sharpest blade cut away everything above the nose.

Their brains, tan, wet, and blood-slick, stood stark, cupped by the shallow edges of their skull basins. The brains pulsed as the sky's tendrils dug deep into them, sucking out something obscured by the tendril's opaque surface.

Albert fell to his knees, coming face to face with the remains of Ms. Daffodil. He shuddered. He couldn't bear the sight of it. His eyes traced up the spire. Tilting back until he saw the point where the sky met the tip. Where the stolen chunks of people disappeared into the heavens.

A thought came to him. As wide and as heavy and as certain as a thought could be.

This isn't over yet.

And when it is, when whatever this is ends, nothing will be left. Nothing happy left.

It won't just kill us.

It'll take everything.

Interlude One

Charley

CHARLEY BRIEFLY WONDERED WHY NO one was buying anything that night. The automatic doors hadn't opened in a long time. He'd forgotten to charge his phone, and it was dead before he woke up that evening. His six-hour night shifts always passed as one long dream without his phone. A blurry linoleum and cheap, overhead light dream. Quiet even with customers. The store wasn't on a major road and didn't sit next to any colleges. His only customers were usually truckers.

There was an old television, but it only got a few channels—and he knew nothing on at this time of night interested him. It was off when he came in, and he didn't bother to change that. Letting the news play would only make the time pass more slowly.

He looked down at his notebook and read what he'd written there the day before. The diagrams were old hat. He'd drawn the basic ideas over and over, but he was always seeing if tweaking it was possible. Once he could afford a game engine good enough, he could test it. He'd get to bring it fully into reality.

Charley hoped people liked it when it was done. He was sure people would enjoy the gameplay he had planned, but the story was basic, and his visuals were not going to win any prizes.

He doodled a basic enemy design, giving it little horns and figuring out how it would run. Then he closed the book. Working on it for too long bummed him out. Also, he risked his boss seeing him slacking off.

Charley cast his eye up to the swiveling camera. His boss, a rather tall and muscular man named Brad, apparently had a way to remotely check the cameras. He doubted Brad was paying attention right this second—he had his own store to run across town—but the chance was still there.

Charley peered out past the counter, checking whether someone was using the gas station. Washing a window. Even just hanging out. Nothing. This was about as dead as it got.

He sat back on the little wooden stool and sighed. Usually, the peace was nice. Today, it was making his skin crawl. The air had an electric anticipation waiting for something to set it off.

Charley looked up at the clock. 3:50 am. He guessed that "something" wasn't going to happen—because his shift was about over. He watched ten minutes take two million years, then got up.

He went to the back of the store, past the meager storage room, and opened the door to the outside.

As expected, Dereck was sitting on the curb, drinking pre-bottled coffee while playing a game on an ancient handheld. Dereck cast his eyes up when Charley stepped out into the too-hot Central California air.

"My turn?" Dereck asked.

"Yep, and I hope you like that game. It's dead quiet," Charley said.

"Is there a charger? I was out of it yesterday. I actually managed to leave my phone here."

"I wish. I would've used it for mine."

"Shit. Oh, well."

Dereck drained the bottle, then stood. Dereck was thin but muscled, his skin extremely tanned from the sun, only pale white on his left wrist. He had a well-cared-for short beard, and his eyes were a light gray, which always caught Charley off guard when they hit the light just right.

"I'll figure something out," Dereck said, stretching his arms above his head. A pair of abs flashed for a second. "You get some sleep, yeah? You look exhausted."

Charley nodded. Tired was not the feeling he was having at the moment.

Dereck walked past him, patting him on the shoulder, and disappeared into the store. For a second, Charley stood still, a blush forming on his face.

He breathed out a few times, trying to dispel the lingering sensation of Dereck's hand.

It mostly worked.

His head was at least clear enough to avoid the glass. Charley stepped onto a parking block to avoid a patch of it. Somehow or another, there was always something busted on the blacktop. Be it a can of soda thrown from some car at high speed or spilled food drawing flies. Or, in this case, a bottle of tequila obliterated into twinkling pieces.

Fortunately, even after all this time, a random projectile had never hit Charley's car. Or, if it had, it hadn't left a dent. Not that his car could look much worse. He'd gotten it from his dad when he didn't need it anymore, and it looked every bit the thirty years it had been on the road. The tires were new, but everything else was beaten up. Its bumpers looked like they might fall off, and on every edge or angle was at least some rust. The paint was flecking, making the once smooth red look like a worn-out, molding apple.

He got in, took one more long breath, then fished his keys out of his pocket. The engine gave only a slightly warped sound as he turned it on. He patted it on the dashboard and pulled it out onto the road.

The lack of sales that night was not a fluke—the streets were also quiet. No cars passed him on the road; the interspersed streetlights made for the only light besides his car.

Charley loved working at night but hated driving in it. He was always so sleepy by this time. Something about the stillness and the simple rumble of his engine made him want to pass out.

But that night, the emptiness kept him going. It was too surreal. He'd almost welcome the odd car waiting alongside the road, dark on the inside. Or even a traffic jam.

Turning onto a side street, he made the roundabout path to his apartment. On the second left, he slowed, ready for the high curb and narrow dirt road.

This place wasn't really made for cars.

It was barely made for buildings.

Whoever planned it had arranged the surrounding houses haphazardly. Some houses were flush with each other, while others helped form a mini network of alleyways. His apartment complex stood as a block in the middle of it. The complex only had about ten units, and the whole structure was made of ugly concrete that looked heavy enough to sink into the open dirt. Most of Charley's neighbors were nice, but the place never felt friendly. The architecture made it seem like it only tolerated humans living in it, glaring down with its many door eyes, willing to outlive its occupants out of sheer spite.

The rent was also cheaper than anything else Charley could find in Bakersfield, and by a lot.

He parked next to the bike rack—bursting with worn bikes and one adult tricycle—and hopped out of his car. He hadn't seen any lights on before, but he still scanned the windows around the complex. Dark. Silent. Everyone was probably asleep this late into the night, but there was almost always *someone* else around. Charley glanced back at the houses. A light was on above someone's porch, but no one was sitting there. Sometimes his insomniac neighbor Darla would be smoking.

He almost yelled something to see if anyone would yell back or if a dog would bark. He was beginning to wonder if he was the only person alive in the whole world right now.

Well, Dereck and him. Maybe something had wiped away all of humanity except those inside the store and its parking lot. Maybe then Charley would get the nerve to ask him out.

He let out a short, bitter chuckle, then unlocked his door. Charley made slightly more noise with the keys than was necessary.

The door stuck, and he shoved it with his shoulder. He hadn't gotten around to asking the landlord about it yet. He could probably watch a video online for instructions once he got his phone charged. Charley bet it had something to do with the frame. It popped open after a second hit.

Once he'd locked the door behind him, he flipped on the light. The overhead's slightly yellow glow washed over his little sanctum. He had an older smart television resting on a bookshelf without books. He'd turned the shelf on its side, so it stretched across a wall. In front of that was a gaming chair with a bright purple ottoman for a footstool. Off by the door to his bedroom was a tiny kitchen and a table with an assortment of chairs that hadn't broken or had comfy cushions. Past that, he had a bed and a desk. The chair pulled double duty, and he pulled it along to his room, knowing perfectly when it would bump on the slight raise in the floor.

He sat down in it heavily, rubbing his eyes. It had taken a long time to admit to himself that he would never have a normal sleep pattern. That, even since high school, he was useless if he had to keep to anything that didn't go deep into the night. But when he got tired, boy, did it hit like a truck.

He turned on his computer and pulled his dead phone out of his pocket. The phone screen had several hairline cracks. He ran his thumb over them: another thing to save up for later. He plugged the phone into the one charging cable he had and put it to the side.

The computer turned on, but the internet was out. He fiddled with the computer's settings, then the modem, mentally checking that, yes, he *had* paid that bill. Restarting did nothing, though.

He shrugged and rolled his eyes. He didn't need the internet for this.

Charley didn't expect to make a living off the game he was working on. He wasn't even sure he wanted to charge for it after release. It was a passion project—a hobby. But, when it came to his game, he had one rule: he had to do something with it every day. That was the only way it was ever getting done.

So, he pulled up his practice code—the stuff to enter into the engine once he had it—and looked for anything that could be improved. He eventually needed to draw assets, but it had taken him so long to learn to code from web videos he felt like checking it over and over again. And learning to make art assets on a computer was extremely daunting.

It came as some shock when his phone vibrated next to him. Several vibrations, actually. The thing inched across the desk, almost falling to the floor.

He grabbed it and turned on the screen. His eyes went wide. Charley had tons of texts, some from people he'd not heard from in years. His ex from high school had texted him. He'd texted if Charley was okay. Seventeen texts came in from his various internet friends. They were all concerned as well.

His father had texted to call him back and called seventeen times within a span of ten minutes. Then once an hour, all night.

There was also a national alert.

A full-on governmental alert.

Panic bloomed in his chest before he could even read it. Nukes? Was it nukes? Were they at war!? Between his tiredness and the thumping in his chest, he couldn't quite get his eyes to focus on it.

NATIONAL ALERT. STAY INDOORS. DO NOT APPROACH FORMATION.

"Don't approach..." he said to himself.

Then he opened the web browser on his phone. Fuck his data plan—he was using a satellite.

It wasn't hard to find pictures. Every vaguely relevant search result brought it up: a giant dark mass, a wall, a cloud, over a huge area. Every picture had some sort of blur, like a classic cryptid snapshot. Charley would've thought it a hoax if it wasn't so widespread—and who was talking about it.

Then he found pictures of people.

Little groups. Streets full. Mobs spanning entire neighborhoods.

And they looked *weird.* One shot showed a person looking right at the camera but not staring. It was more like they happened to be looking that way while day-dreaming. They were slouching and had their arms hanging loosely at their sides.

"*... what some doctors are calling a 'dangerous sudden onset of malaise.'*"

"*We're getting nationwide reports of intense lethargy. In some cases, the patients have been losing the ability to speak or stand. They'll just turn out the lights, go to bed, and that's it.*"

"*The president is urging citizens to stay away from the formation. To seek whatever shelter is available as the situation develops. If your loved ones are affected, make sure they stay hydrated and fed.*"

Charley's eyes darted from article to article, not fully reading any of them. The back of his head buzzed with anxious energy. This couldn't be real. Something this big couldn't be happening.

His eyes fell on one of the headlines.

This *couldn't* be fucking real.

Quill Point, Illinois.

He grabbed his phone and found her number in his contacts. As it rang, he looked for texts from her among the panicked ones. Nothing.

"Hello, you've reached Cassy. Leave a message or whatever."

"Cassy, call me back!" Charley yelled into the phone.

He hung up. Then tried again. Each time it went to voice mail. He shot off multiple texts. Nothing was happening. His hands got slick with sweat, and he kept wiping them on his pant legs.

After ten tries, he switched tactics.

"Dad?"

"Oh my god, you're okay! I was… are you okay?"

"I'm fine. I'm fine. I didn't even know. My phone was just off. Dad, why isn't Cassy answering? Is she with you?"

"No, I can't get through to her."

Charley looked at the screen again, reading that headline. Seeing that cloud the size of a town. A horrible sensation was pressing against his stomach. He was pretty sure the stress was going to make him puke.

"Is she still living in Quill Point?"

"Yes… I don't…"

The sound on the other end was hard to parse at first. And not just because the connection wasn't great. It was because Charley had only heard his father cry twice. Once when Charley's uncle didn't come back from active service, and once after he got a compound fracture building a cement block outbuilding.

"Dad, where are you?"

"I'm…" His breath came out in a staticky hiss. "I'm at the home. They have us staying in our rooms. I keep hearing sirens, but I don't know what's happening."

Charley breathed in and out too fast to bring in much actual air. His mind worked harder than it had in a long time. There were so many factors, all swirling. His dad was in assisted living in Indiana. He had a mostly full tank of gas, but not a lot of money to buy more. It could take up to three days to get there, depending on how much he slept—depending on how crowded or empty the streets were.

And what other shit could be happening out there?

But if it was the end of the world…

There really wasn't a choice, was there?

If there was a chance to get to his family before whatever happened next, he would take it. If he could help his sister, he would do it.

Cassandra would do the same for him.

"I'll be there as fast as I can, Dad."

"What!?"

"I'm coming to get you."

"But … it could be dangerous."

"Yes," Charley said. "But I'm coming there to get you, okay?"

"I don't…"

"If not for you, then for Cassy, okay?" Charley said.

There was a long pause. In the background, Charley could hear a police cruiser get close, then speed away somewhere.

"Okay."

"I love you."

"I love you, too."

Charley hung up. He stood in his empty apartment that now felt too large. He looked around his bedroom with quick glances. Charley hadn't done laundry in a while. So, no clean clothes to pack. He hadn't cooked recently either—so going to the fridge was a non-starter.

Also, he had nothing remotely close to a travel bag. Trips had seemed like such a ridiculous idea to even entertain.

Fucking hell.

He ran to the kitchen and opened the cabinet underneath his sink. It was stuffed with plastic grocery bags from places that hadn't switched to paper or reusable.

It had felt wrong to throw them out—and now he finally had a use for them.

His clothes smelled vaguely of sweat or ketchup, and he wasn't sure which was worse. He stuffed them down into the bags and tied them off. All of his clothing filled five, almost to bursting.

It wasn't that physically taxing, but he was still out of breath when he finished. He bit his lip. The panic sitting in his body refused to numb even a little. He couldn't stop seeing the hollow, sunken look of those people in the articles.

He cast his gaze upward. The apartment above his had two people living there. A nice couple—they'd even brought him a six-pack of beer when he moved in.

He had a feeling they were up there now, sitting in the dark. Or lying down. Or dying slowly, staring like zombies. The articles hadn't made it clear how many people had whatever this was—they likely didn't know—but it was everywhere.

It felt like he *should've* gotten more warning than this. That the end of the world needed more windup. A series of escalations, a chance to wonder and worry. Hoaxes, false starts, and days of panic. Not the world getting hit like this; everything turning different overnight.

Charley swallowed back tears and started moving the clothing bags to his car. They fit in his trunk with plenty of space to go. He ran back to see what else he could get. The single cup of ancient forgotten apple sauce in his fridge wouldn't last much longer, so he chugged it down.

It was possible he would need to get used to eating whatever he could find.

He pulled out a baseball bat from the back of his closet, swung it once, then stowed it in his car as well. Next, he grabbed his notebook and then picked up his entire computer. There wasn't time to pull data off it. Once the computer was secured in his car, he took one more look inside his apartment.

"Fuck," he said quietly.

Cassy needed him. She was infinitely more important than the apartment. It was stuff, walls, and not even a nice place. But it was his, and he had worked for it, and now he would probably never see it again.

Charley closed the door and locked it. The outside world was still so silent. But as he looked around, he imagined lethargic people staring back at him through the walls. Each house could have any number of people trapped inside them.

He breathed as evenly as he could.

A twinkling sound startled him. He fumbled out his phone, expecting it to be his father.

It wasn't. It was the store's number. The profile picture was Dereck wearing a company-approved snapback and muscle shirt. He was holding the free extra-large drink he had gotten for his first month working there.

Charley answered it.

"Holy fucking shit," was the immediate response.

"Are you okay?" Charley asked.

"I'm okay," Dereck replied. "But holy shit. Is this fake? I turned on the television ... and it was just the same words over and over. There's a channel... there's a broadcast from the fucking White House. Is this really happening?"

"It's really happening," Charley heard himself saying. Although he felt far away from himself as he did.

"Fucking Christ. I..."

"Listen, I need to... I'm not sure what to do. But stay indoors."

"Are you okay!?" Dereck said.

"I'm fine. I just need to go somewhere. I need to—"

"What? Why?"

Charley's mouth felt very dry. It was already nightmarish to consider the full scope of what he was doing and what was happening. But to say it aloud?

"I need to go to my family," was the safest way to put it. "I need to go see them."

"Oh, shit." Dereck's voice was very quiet.

"Yeah. I'm going to go to Indiana. I... I don't know what else to do."

"Let me come with," Dereck blurted.

"What?" Charley said.

"You're going to go across the country alone?"

"I need to—"

"I'm coming with. I'll be there in five minutes. I don't think I'm finishing my shift."

Charley made a sound somewhere between surprise, sorrow, and a laugh. A shift. A *shift*? How quickly did that word feel alien and absurd?

Charley looked at his car, at the beaten-up car. At the empty seat. And imagined the huge stretch of unknown between where he was and where his father and sister were. And all he had was a bat.

"Charley?" Dereck said.

"Okay," Charley said. "Yeah ... okay, just get here fast. We need to... we need to get going. Uh, do you have a gun?"

"I bet you the boss keeps one somewhere around here. In case someone tries to take the register."

Charley then noticed the taste of apples still clinging to his tongue. "Actually, I'm coming there."

"Okay… sure," Dereck said.

Charley's racing mind locked onto something. Apocalypse movies. Somehow, that was the world now. And there was usually a scene in those movies where the characters raided a food store. A scene where they got a lot of tools, equipment, and junk food.

"Yeah, I'm coming there. I think we may need to use our, uh, employee discount. We can pay him back later or something. Work it off…"

"You want to steal all the food?"

"Yeah. I do."

"It's really that bad, isn't it?" Dereck asked.

"Yeah. I think, uh, I think the whole world might just be fucked."

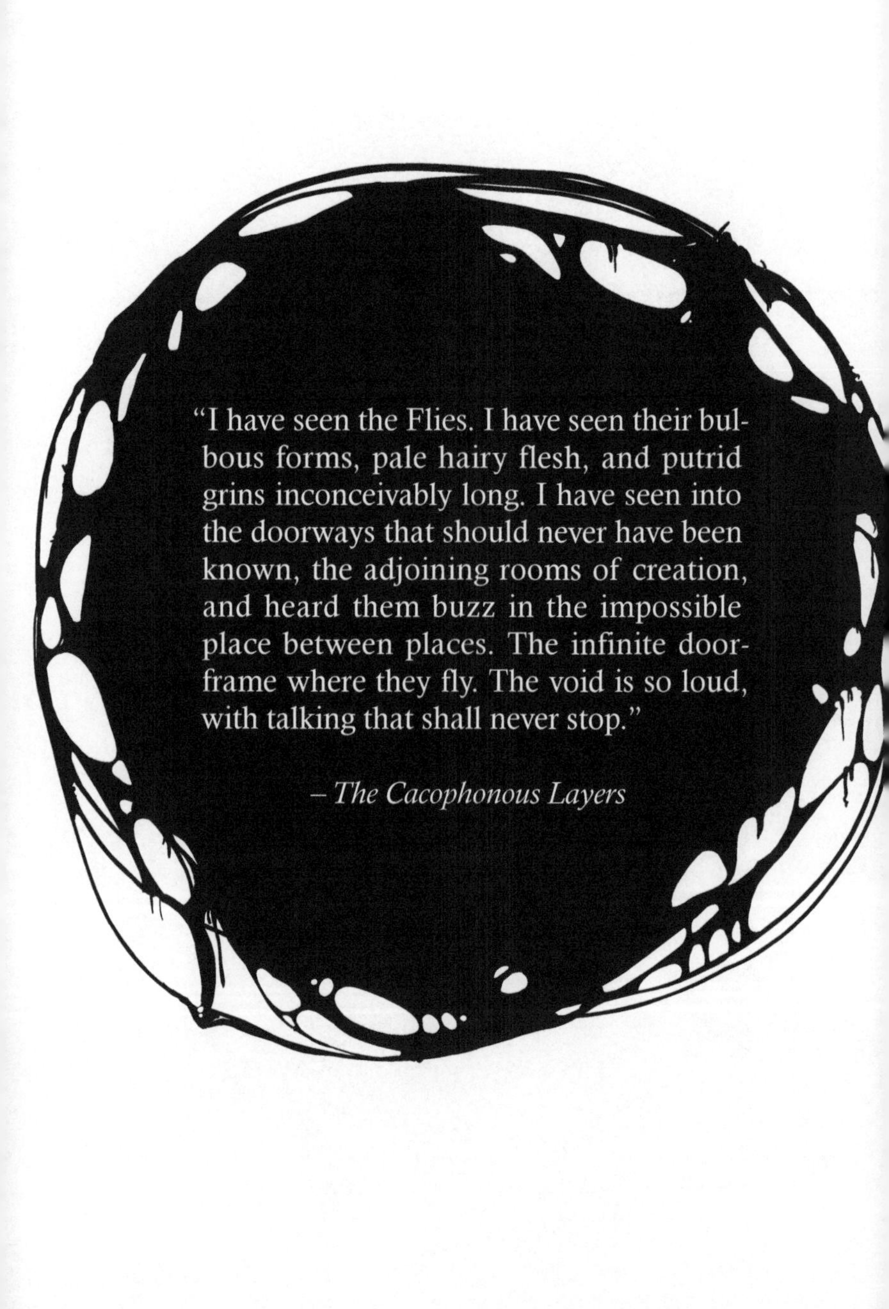

"I have seen the Flies. I have seen their bulbous forms, pale hairy flesh, and putrid grins inconceivably long. I have seen into the doorways that should never have been known, the adjoining rooms of creation, and heard them buzz in the impossible place between places. The infinite doorframe where they fly. The void is so loud, with talking that shall never stop."

– *The Cacophonous Layers*

Part 2

Immortalized in Clay

Chapter Seven

Bree was artistically blocked, and the ceiling of the Kraken Hotel offered no inspiration. All she could think about was Murder Sky. Bree rarely got a chance to talk to anyone her own age—certainly not in lower income brackets—but she'd heard that was the nickname for it. She assumed it was the devil, but aliens weren't an uncommon assertion.

Whatever it was, the feeling of it still sat in her chest. When she closed her eyes, she heard the snap of wood. The crash. The oak tree from her childhood playtime taking out her bedroom armoire. Several of her creations exploding into powder. A bruise by her left eye hadn't fully healed yet.

At times like these, she almost missed her father, the mayor. If nothing else, he made her feel safer. Financially, certainly, but also, the cops were so close by they could make it to her old house in under five minutes on a hectic traffic day.

But he was still mad at her for yelling at him during the town meeting. She was sure of it. He was staying in his office, and she was rotting in this hotel room. It was amazing how fast mundanity came back, even when things were wrong. It was amazing that she could still be bored when the world might be ending.

Bree groaned and rubbed at her eyes, then twirled her multicolored hair around her finger. The ceiling was such a dull color—an ocean green that reminded her of puked-up seaweed. Usually, when she was blocked, she would use her cell phone and stare at social media. That obviously wasn't an option anymore. She might even be failing to fulfill online orders—assuming the world still existed elsewhere.

Bree stretched out on the king-sized bed and attempted to reach her toes and fingers to all four corners. It didn't work. She tried again, and her back hurt.

"All right, fine," Bree said and sat up.

She looked with open disdain at the half-formed statue sitting on the only table in the hotel room. Bree had been finicking with it for the longest time. It refused to look the way she wanted it to. It scoffed at her attempts.

But the sculpture would have to listen to her today. Or she would throw it out the window. Then collect it again. She had only enough raw clay to do five small projects. She couldn't even bake it, just mold it. All she was really doing was practicing.

She scooted to the edge of her bed and found her slippers. She'd somehow had the sense of mind to get slippers when she'd dug through the rubble of her house. They were shaped like little crocodiles and ate her feet as she put them on one at a time.

Bree knew she was stalling—but she also had so much time. The sky hung like a dark monster, but did nothing. People mostly stayed where they were. Cars weren't on the roads anymore.

Her world was shut down, and all she had was time.

And it turned out that unlimited time wasn't her friend.

Bree had always said that if she had more time, that if there was nothing else to do, she would get so much art done. But that turned out to be a complete lie. Deadlines got art done, not the muse, not unfettered creativity.

And, to top it off, terror at the state of the world didn't exactly make her want to create beautiful things.

Mostly, Bree felt tired.

But tiredly, she walked to the table, sat down, and inspected what she'd done the previous day.

She'd been making busts. Little busts, about the size of her fist, with the faces of people she'd met around the hotel. Currently, the one she was working on was the hotel's receptionist. Her name was Milda. A woman a little older than her with the shiniest blond hair Bree had ever seen. She had a distinct severity to the arc of her face that didn't gel with her sweet demeanor. It didn't go with her smile, either, framed by a pink complexion and a mild tan. Maybe that contrast, that smile that changed her whole face, was why she was having such trouble recreating it. She hadn't seen it in a while.

The thing she'd managed was simply a crude outline of a face. No eyes, no nose, just a lopsided and ill-constructed grin. Every time she tried to do more, she would stop and frown. Horrible jittery energy would go into her fingers. A clenched hand would engulf her brain. She could do better than what she was about to do; she knew it.

She gritted her teeth and pushed past the sensation. She used her thumbs to give it indentations that could become eyes.

Then she wiped it all away with a slash of her hand and stood up.

"You don't want to be finished, do you?!"

The clay obviously didn't answer.

Bree put her head in her hands. Pictured Milda. Saw her face. Her hair. Saw her in such a way she could capture more of her than a photograph.

The image was too fuzzy. She closed her eyes harder—willing clarity by flexing some unknowable muscle. She kept tightening her eyes until she let out a little annoyed gasp. Her shoulders and jaw hurt.

"Okay, fucking fine," she said.

Bree grabbed her bathrobe, slipped it over her pink pajamas, stomped to the hotel door, then paused. She pursed her lips and gently spun the handle. She peeked in one direction, then the other. As usual, everyone was in their rooms, doing whatever people without the internet did for hours and hours.

Bree was worried that *she* would pop up and talk to her. The little girl who lived three rooms down.

She was fairly young, no older than ten. She had a pale white complexion, brown eyes, and black hair that was always messy. Whenever Bree ran into her, she'd smile, revealing a missing tooth. And she was always very keen on playing around with Bree's clay. At first, when Bree met the little girl, it seemed like a good thing: another artist she could help. A budding talent to encourage. But the girl really only wanted to play with clay. Wanted to make little crude people, then smash them with her hands.

And Bree could only tolerate that for so long. She liked kids well enough, but being around them for too long sucked all the energy out of her. It made her grouchy.

So, the only solution, clearly, was to hide from the little girl as much as possible.

Which wasn't exactly easy when the girl had literally nothing better to do.

But no one seemed around. So, Bree slipped out of her room. She held her breath as she crept along—hoping against hope that the floor wouldn't creak. Hoping the old building didn't make any old building sounds.

She kept on scanning, but wanted to close her eyes. The hotel was the ugliest building she'd ever seen. If an interior designer walked into the place, they would detonate—explode into little chunks with enough force to *maybe* paint the walls a better color.

The main issue was the carpets and walls were a similar awful green as her room's ceiling, just slightly different shades. The visible wood was yellowish, old, and seemed somehow washed out. It was like walking across a tableau of spoiled bread.

Another issue was the statue they'd erected a few feet from the top of the stairs to the bottom floor. It was the same gray color as the railing and was done so poorly that it made her eyes twitch.

The statue was of a woman holding a quill. Bree had seen pictures of the town founder, Irena Ink, and this was as if she'd been petrified, then melted. Her chin was oddly angular, like a bone cracked in the wrong direction.

If Bree had any real political power, she would remove this thing in a heartbeat. But, like a lot of the uglier things in the town, they were a matter of tradition—older than her by double or more and allowed to exist no matter what.

Her slippers made no sound as she went down the first few steps of the staircase. She glanced up to make sure the little girl wasn't following her. Still nothing. Bree made it to the bottom unscathed, holding her breath the whole way.

Milda spotted her pretty much right away. Her gaze snapped up from the book she was reading, and a smile spread quickly across her face.

Bree smiled back. It was hard not to. Bree not only thought Milda was pretty in the same way a well-crafted sculpture was, but she radiated similar tranquility. It was hard not to get swept into it. Milda spent hour after hour at that desk, basically never leaving since Murder Sky, and never seemed to mind.

Bree looked up at the railing once more, then sighed. She walked slowly over to Milda.

"Still avoiding the little one?" Milda whispered.

"I just haven't been up for high energy lately."

Milda gently nodded at that.

That was the other thing Bree liked about her: she never seemed to question anything you said. Sometimes it was hard to tell if she'd been fully listening with how much she took the oddest things in stride. Bree had once spent a solid half-hour explaining the formation of a human torso and how she'd modeled it with clay—even the rib-cage and organs—and Milda had just nodded along and asked the occasional question.

"What are you reading?" Bree asked, breaking the somehow still comfortable silence.

Milda held up a paperback. It was a stylized and simplistic rendering of a couple kissing. It consisted of bright primary colors and simple shapes to make up the two leads and their city background.

"A romance novel. It's decent." Milda put it next to the other books she had hidden underneath the countertop. "I've certainly read worse."

Bree leaned forward and stood on her tiptoes to see the pile. Milda's reading habits were always interesting.

The pile was about five books high. Besides the romance novel, Bree could see a cover with bloody letters and a girl screaming at someone holding a hammer. The paper was older, pulpy, and well-loved.

Bree quirked up her eyebrow and dropped back down.

"Uh, that's an interesting choice there," Bree said.

"It helps," Milda replied.

"It does?"

In a rare break from form, Milda grimaced. "Yeah, it does. Have you seen it?"

Bree didn't have to ask what she meant. The Prayer Spire.

"Only once," Bree said.

"How close did you get?" Milda asked, tilting her head.

A shiver shot up Bree's spine. She grimaced and looked off at nothing in particular. The memory was fresh—it came almost unbidden. She'd been pulled to stand right in front of it like everyone else. It tugged at the pit of your stomach and made you want to stay there forever.

She'd cried in front of it for two hours.

"Very close."

"I was a little bit away. I was walking with my partner. Seeing how the officers were setting up the tent circles for the people who lost their houses. I had to hold back my dog when we got too close to it. My dog kept growling at it. I started reading this stuff again after that."

"Didn't know you had a dog," Bree said.

Milda just shrugged.

"So," Bree continued, "something scary helps you?"

"I used to do it when I was a kid," Milda said. A smile slowly migrated back onto her face, and that tranquility flowed back in.

Bree realized she'd just gotten what she wanted. The perfect expression to render in clay: a soft smile that held a touch of nostalgia. She tried to hold on to it.

"I used to watch this one vampire movie," Milda continued. "It was the cheesiest thing. Huge plastic fangs in the actor's mouth—I could barely tell what he was saying. But I was a little kid, so it scared me. I couldn't even look when he drank someone's blood. The thing was, once I calmed down and watched it for a little while, the thing that had been worrying me all day didn't anymore."

"What was it that worried you?"

Milda gently laughed. "I don't even remember."

"Oh," Bree said.

Milda reached over to the pile of books and pulled out another. The cover had something made of goo and teeth chasing a couple framed by headlights. She flipped through the pages.

"And then it clicked for me. A book can go anywhere. So, when I'm scared, when it's scary out there, I can scare myself here. I can make it not so bad. Haven works at that little bookstore, Stylus Books. They like reading horror on their breaks, so sometimes they recommend stuff I'll like. It really does help certain types of people."

"Well, I'm glad it works for you."

Milda held out the book. "Would you like to try? I'm betting you get really bored up there."

With everything going on, Bree couldn't imagine subjecting herself to stories of monsters. The romance novel was more interesting. Bree didn't experience those sorts of feelings, but the stories could still be fun to read.

But she already had what she needed from Milda.

Now she needed to make art, not experience someone else's.

"I'm fine," Bree said, frowning slightly.

"Oh, okay," Milda said, putting the book back on her pile.

Bree felt a slight stab of regret. That was rude of her.

"Maybe later, though," Bree added hastily. "If you end up reading any fantasy, I'd probably like those a lot more."

"High fantasy or low fantasy?" Milda asked.

Bree pursed her lips. She didn't really know subgenres. Books weren't her thing. She'd chosen her artistic pursuit; she didn't want to get tempted to make another.

"Uh, something with, like, elves," she said.

"Okay," Milda said. She leaned forward on the counter. "Haven's coming by later to visit; I'll ask them to check the store for something you'd like."

"Thanks," Bree said.

When Milda said nothing more, Bree walked away. That was the usual way that conversations ended with Milda. She seemed comfortable with silence—didn't mind if you came and went.

After a few steps, Bree slowed down to sneak to her room. The carpet felt vaguely like a minefield.

She shouldn't have bothered. As soon as she made it halfway up the stairs, she saw the girl sitting on one of the chairs dotting the second floor. She swung her legs back and forth. Her gaze was so glued to her shoes that Bree was almost convinced she hadn't spotted her.

But then, as if Bree had thought too loudly, the little girl's head snapped up. She smiled widely—in the center of that smile was a dark hole where a tooth would eventually be.

"Hi there, Bree!" the little girl said. "May you please show me more sculpting?"

Bree sighed under her breath. The inspiration was still so *fresh*. But it felt wrong to deny a kid. The world *was* ending. How could she possibly be mean to her?

Bree bit back a groan and smiled.

"Yeah, come on. I'll let you try something with the clay, all right?"

Chapter Eight

"Why do you make things?" the girl asked.

She was pushing together a lump of clay. She'd made a few crude shapes and was now slowly smashing them into a blob.

Bree had been sitting across from her for the last ten minutes, occasionally offering her advice. She didn't know why she kept trying. The little girl would immediately destroy or warp the things Bree helped her make. Bree was beginning to wonder if this was all a trick to get unpaid babysitting.

"Brianna?"

Bree snapped out of her thoughts. "What?"

"Why do you make things? What do you like about it?"

Bree had too many answers. It was because it had made her mom smile during the worst parts of the divorce. Because the last time she'd called, almost two years ago now, she'd told Bree to keep going at her art. It was because a teacher had seen talent in her and tried to encourage it. It was because of, well…

Well, there had to be a diplomatic way to say *that* reason.

"Well, okay. I make these sculptures because they last longer than me."

"Sculptures break," the girl said. She slammed her fist down on the clay blob, making a dent.

"They do, but they last a really long time when they don't. Here, let me show you something."

Bree got up and grabbed her phone. She'd had the same background for the past five years.

"Okay, so, see this? It's from a church, and it's hundreds of years old. We *still* have art from then. We might not know the names of the people who made them all, but we remember that the art exists. I don't care if they remember my name as long as someone likes my statues."

"Are you scared to die?" the girl asked.

Bree flinched. "Everyone is."

The girl looked down and twisted up stalks in the clay. A pensive look formed, like she was solving a puzzle. She made a weird shape by connecting the stalks. Then the little girl smashed it down with her hand and molded a simple head. She pushed her thumbs into the clay, making two crude eyes.

"I'm not afraid to die," the girl declared. She smiled like she'd answered a question right on a quiz.

"Okay," Bree said.

"I don't think I will either, actually."

Bree didn't feel like correcting her on that.

"No, really. I won't," the girl said, looking at Bree.

Her gaze was remarkably steady. Bree couldn't help but entertain the notion, for just a second, that she knew what she was talking about.

"I said 'okay,'" Bree replied.

"I'll get this superpower, like ... uh..."

"Someone from a cartoon you saw?" Bree asked, leaning forward.

"No, not from that. I think it's called 'immortality.'"

"That does mean not dying," Bree replied.

"Yeah, that. I won't die. I won't break."

She looked down at the clay. And she got this *smirk*. Then she slammed her hand into the clay repeatedly. It flattened out across the table. It inched past the plastic that Bree had put down.

Before she could ruin the hotel table with stains, Bree reached out and stopped her hand. The little girl was surprisingly strong, and Bree's wrist smacked into the wood hard enough for her to wince.

"Oh, sorry," the girl said. She looked at Bree's hand strangely.

All the hairs on the back of Bree's neck stood on end. Bree snatched her hand back and pushed herself away from the table.

The girl looked up at her with a level gaze. It was flat, stoic.

"I think I'm going to go now," she said. "Thanks for letting me learn about clay, Bree. I think I finally know how I'm going to do the next step."

"Uh, you're welcome."

"Don't be afraid to die, Bree," she said cheerfully.

"Okay... I won't?"

"There's always the chance you'll be a special one, right? Maybe *you* can learn not to die as I will. Maybe you can survive."

Bree's entire body was tensing up. "What are you talking about?"

"Some people will have to survive, you know. Not everyone can die. Otherwise, what's the point? Just put up a good fight, so no one suspects I'm rooting for you, okay?"

"I don't understand...?" Bree said.

But her mind was already racing. Why had she never even thought to ask this girl her name? Where were her parents? Why had they never once even checked on her?

Why did it feel like a train was barreling toward her?

"Wait!" Bree shouted.

The girl smiled and stood. She moved far too fast. Or maybe Bree was slowing down. Her hand, reaching out over the table, moved in slow motion. The little girl started to hum a song with a tune that sounded somehow both discordant and orchestral.

She turned, flung open the door, then stepped over the threshold.

When she looked back, her face was off. Her eyes were—

Oh god, what was wrong with her face?

—the door closed.

A slap of invisible force pushed outward. All the hair on Bree's head and arms stood up for a second. Then, she was flung out of her chair. She crashed to the ground, her slippers sliding off her feet.

A headache bloomed behind Bree's eyes, and she panted as she lay there. The air stank of something earthy and sour. That ugly, ugly ceiling looked down at her as she blinked away floaters.

"What the fuck?" she said, rolling onto her stomach. "What is happening?"

She stood up and walked to the door. Bree wasn't sure she wanted to follow that little girl. But she for sure didn't want to be in the hotel anymore. Something supernatural was happening again. She needed to get somewhere safer.

Only the door wouldn't open.

She tugged harder, and it remained completely still.

Panic spiraled out from the center of her gut, and she threw her body into the pull. The door didn't even groan. Her breath quickened. Only now did she notice that the door hinges were caked with a thick collection of her own clay. It covered the whole outline of the door with a perfect seal.

It moved slightly, puffing from some unseen air. The clay looked almost alive, like a fungus or tumor.

She put her whole body into one more tug. Her arms screamed with pain. Bree looked down. Her hands were red and raw, with flecks of the handle's paint dotting her palm.

"Help!"

She leaned as close to the door's hinge as she could without touching it. Its layer of clay looked too thick to allow sound. She tried anyway.

"Can anyone hear me?!"

The clay pulsed out again, almost brushing her nose.

Bree grimaced and pulled back. After a second of thinking, she gritted her teeth and tore at it with her fingernails. It didn't feel like clay anymore. It was chunkier, slimier.

It got under her fingernails and pulsed at her attacks. Where she tore, it breathed out flowing clay to seal the openings. Bree's fingertips were bleeding. She tossed chunks of the clay behind her with frantic swings of her hands.

"Someone, please help me!"

Her arms burned, a deep ache already starting. She stopped, breathing hard. The clay quickly undid all of her efforts.

It was hard to hear at first, but as her breathing calmed, she could detect something behind her. Frantic tapping sounds. It was like quarters dropping into a vending machine: continuous, rhythmic, and incessant.

A shiver shot up her spine. The pain in her fingers increased sharply. Bree glanced at her hands in alarm. The clay underneath her nails was expanding. It was pushing up at the undersides.

The tapping sounds grew louder. Bree almost turned her head when a deep feeling told her not to. A primal warning shot through her skull: *do not look.* Her breathing got sharper. Spit was piling up in her throat. She had to swallow it down to even breathe.

Her gaze instead fell on the bathroom floor. A towel she'd not bothered to hang up the last time she'd taken a shower was sitting in a little crumpled pile. That towel looked completely surreal to Bree. It was totally out of step with how the world had suddenly become. But it was in a room that had a door, and that door *locked*.

She took a single step toward the bathroom.

The tapping shifted up in pitch. Then became a wet rumble.

Bree bolted for the door.

A guttural, phlegmy scream came from behind her. It was not human. It was not an animal. Her body told her it would kill her.

Feet pounded behind Bree, running right at her. She skidded into the bathroom and slammed the door as hard as she could. A wet thud slammed into the other side. The door handle yanked downward before she could lock it.

Another strangled and otherworldly cry came, and immense pressure pushed on the door. Bree was whimpering completely involuntarily and pushing back as hard as she could.

"Please, no," she breathed.

Pulsing slams from the other side came again and again. Bree gritted her teeth so hard it felt like she could shatter them.

A bone-breaking shove came next. The wood buckled, sending Bree's bare feet skidding against the linoleum floor. Immediate and sharp pain spiked across her ankle and the soles of her feet. She threw her body forward at the door, catching it as it opened a crack.

She wasn't fast enough. A pair of huge finger-like appendages, easily longer than a forearm, coiled around the wood. They snapped divots into it with gunshot-loud cracks. Bree screamed. She pushed into the door, trying to sever them.

She was fighting a losing battle. Adrenaline only worked for so long.

More appendages slid into the room. The skin was gray and covered in indentations.

Bree howled in desperation, leaning in as hard as she could. Her entire body was hurting—but her fingers were the worst. The clay had grown even more, and entire nails were being pushed off her hands.

Another tremendous shove. The gap widened. A head leaned around the opening.

Bree screamed again.

It was clay. It was the little girl's crude sculpture, without a mouth, without a true face. Only those crude eyes stared at her.

"Go away!" Bree found herself shouting. She saw only condemnation in those thumb marks. "Please!"

The tentacles tightened, and splinters coated the floor.

"Please!" Bree screamed.

The figure shifted its head back out of sight. Bree gasped and pushed. It didn't matter why the reprieve came, just that it did. Her toes tightened against the slippery surface of the linoleum as she shoved. The tentacle hand retracted, and the door closed. She clicked the lock, leaning her head against the remaining door, trying to catch her breath.

And then the hinges snapped with a metal pop.

The entire door was pulled away from her.

Bree's arms shot out to either side, catching herself on the doorframe.

The sculpture, now taller than a fully grown person, stood with legs made of coiled lines. It had a mess of tentacles where its arms would be. A chest made of slithering connections. An enlarged version of the girl's creation sat at the top like a bulbous rock.

Some part of Bree's brain, the part that had taken anatomy classes, recognized it as the same structure as the human nervous system.

It stepped forward, its many nerve arms coiling and sliding toward her. She stumbled back, unable to get her mouth to produce any more screams. She didn't look behind her and fell into the tub, slamming her head against the tiled wall. A horrible white light flashed in her eyes. A burst bulb of pain accompanied it. She gasped and blinked rapidly. Through a fog, she could see the figure bend down over her, the lines of clay forming a trap of twisting branches.

Bree kicked out at the tentacles, only for one to catch her leg and lift it up into the air.

"No! No!" she yelled.

She desperately grabbed for something.

She scooped up a roll of toilet paper off the top of the toilet and lobbed it at the creature's head. It did nothing. She jerked off the tank lid, but it was too heavy and clattered out of her hands.

The tentacles of clay wrapped around her leg, digging into the skin.

She shifted her body any which way she could, trying to escape. Trying to get an opening. Her hand fell on the towel. The old towel she'd showered with. It was still damp.

She slapped it into the side of the creature's head.

It stumbled. A part of its face looked looser, more disconnected. She whipped it again, and a solid dent formed. The tentacles loosened, and Bree dropped slightly, her lower hip smacking into the bathtub. She barely registered it.

She gathered the towel to herself, and a huge amount of its clay skin had stuck to the wet parts.

The monster seemed to have composed itself and was moving, albeit more slowly, to grab her.

Bree looked up at the handle for the shower. Without considering what she was doing, she pulled on it, and the water crashed into the creature's front. It shrank back immediately, large rivets and chunks of its body falling off.

Bree sprang up, almost slipping. She whipped the towel at it over and over and over, screaming obscenities with each swing. The fabric grew thicker with collected clay and the pounding water. The monster collapsed into chunks, thick rivulets going down the drain. When it was only a layer of sludge on the floor of the tub, she dropped to her knees and scrapped it into the drain with the towel, not daring to touch it.

When it was all gone, rinsed away to nothing, she stared down the drain, breathing hard. The water slowly grew colder against her back. Her eyes could barely focus, and her head was pounding. But she kept looking until she was sure it wouldn't rise back out of the drain. Her hands shook from pain and exhaustion, but she managed to shut off the shower.

She almost passed out. Instead, she exhaustedly watched blood trickle off her fingers.

At least the clay was gone.

Shifting in the wet tub, she leaned on the edge and let her legs splay out. She was *so* cold. Her pajamas and bathrobe were both soaked through, heavy and uncomfortable against her skin.

The sobbing tears hit her next. The emotions came in as the shock and the adrenaline faded from her body. She hugged herself.

She sat like that for a few moments, but managed to steady her breathing when it occurred to her that the one she killed might not be the only monster. She held her breath, straining to hear more wet, horrible noises. Nothing came to her.

Swallowing back a wince and then almost another sob, she shifted in the bathtub. Bree used the side of her hand and the middle of her palm to reach over to a cabinet. She pried it open slowly. She dragged out a package of adhesive bandages and rubbing alcohol.

Using the edges of her wrists, she picked up both and placed them in front of her. She stared at them wearily, with dread slamming into her stomach. She knew what she had to do. And it was going to *fucking hurt*.

Hands shaking, she picked up the bottle of rubbing alcohol. Her breath grew unsteady. She spread out her nondominant hand, wincing at the sight of the puckered, angry skin.

Bree counted down for herself, jaw tightening with each number.

Then she tipped the alcohol over her hand—

And screamed *bloody murder*.

The agonizing, white-hot pain made her almost pass out. She pulled her hand to her chest, cradling it as each open wound flared with mind-cracking pain.

Bree was crying again. Stuttering shrieks and long, barely restrained screams echoed out from her throat. She applied bandages to each swollen, red finger, barely able to coordinate the action.

Then she looked at her other hand.

And reached for the bottle.

Chapter Nine

BREE STOOD AT THE STILL-SEALED DOOR. She had a newly wet towel in one hand and the room's curtain rod in the other. Getting the rod had been horrible. On the other side of her window was a wall of clay. Clay that moved and slid in such a way it had a face and was opening its mouth so very wide.

She didn't dare open the window.

She'd wrapped five layers of bandages over her fingers, yet it still hurt to lift the towel and scrub at the clay holding the door closed. Like with the monster before, it dissolved cleanly and dripped down to the floor in disgusting rivulets. It didn't grow back when she went to clean the towel. The door was just the door.

She reached to open the door, only to pause. Maybe it was best to stay in the room. Maybe her dad would send the police to help her.

Then again, they hadn't been able to stop the sky from taking people.

Behind her came a soft, barely audible moan.

She didn't need to look to know where it was coming from. Bree yanked at the handle. It opened with a soft pop, like an airtight seal. She could immediately hear screaming.

It wasn't one voice or a crowd. It was sporadic bursts of human fear. One nearby, one far away. Then another about two rooms over from her. Each didn't last long. Each abruptly stopped.

But Bree barely paid attention to it once she'd fully opened the door.

It wasn't the hotel anymore. The architecture was the same. The doors were still where they'd been. But it was *wrong*. The walls were covered in thick layers of clay. But it wasn't simply *on* the wall; it was a part of the wall. Infesting the wall.

Like paths of carpenter ants, there were hands of clay. They crawled in lines, never touching, never intersecting, but made the entire space feel like it was shifting. Every so often, they passed a point where a solid mass of clay grew out of the wall like a hornet's nest.

As Bree looked over the hotel, a man ran by.

He stumbled as he did, screaming for help.

Bree recognized him, though only from passing. Mr. Summers. He worked at the bank, and Bree didn't know his first name. They'd chatted once or twice when the hotel served breakfast. Bree opened her mouth to say something.

A clay monster barreled up behind Mr. Summers. Loping, striding, its strange tentacle legs sliding in perfect tandem.

Before Bree could even move to help, it caught him.

It didn't grab him like it did Bree; it enveloped him. Its chest cavity opened, and its various tentacles lashed around Mr. Summers. He fell backward, struggling as it pulled. As soon as the cavity's lips passed over the top of his head, the monster bent forward.

It tilted further, further, bending its clay head towards its clay feet. Mr. Summers disappeared from sight.

But Bree could still hear him yelling, then howling in pain. Cascading cracks fired off. They were dry at first, then wetter. A single burst of blood shot out of the closing cavity. Mr. Summers stopped screaming quickly.

The monster continued to fold itself up, eventually tucking itself into a large ball.

Bree's pulse hammered in her ears, hands, and stomach. She swallowed back the bile rising in her throat. The feeling kept building. After a few seconds, she vomited on the ground.

Bree wiped her mouth with the towel and stopped looking at the clay ball.

"I have to…" she muttered.

Bree took a single step out, and another scream came from somewhere. Probably within a hotel room. Bree managed to only flinch. Somehow, nothing seemed to notice her yet. She just needed to stay quiet. Needed to not scream, no matter what she saw.

The carpet, blissfully, wasn't alive with clay. Small piles were around and seemed to breathe, but they didn't react as she skirted past them. In her mind's eye, Bree kept picturing her goal. She needed to get to the front door.

Down the stairs. Past reception. Out the door.

Each step was trudging. With each step, she cast her gaze around. She kept expecting a monster made of clay to run at her and snap her neck. But it was quiet and still. The only sounds were the extremely unpleasant shuffling of the clay hands. They made little thumps when the palms hit the wall.

Still, it was better than the screams.

Bree didn't like thinking about *why* they'd stopped.

She made it to the lip of the stairs. Then she caught something in the corner of her eye and jolted. She held the curtain rod up to smack it. But it was just the statue of Irena Ink. Bree still eyed it for another moment, fully prepared for it to move. When it remained immobile, she let out a steadying breath and took another step down the stairs.

After a second, she looked back.

It wasn't quite the same statue.

For one, her face looked worried, afraid. For another, it looked way more like the pictures Bree had seen most of her life. There was a level of detail that not even the greatest sculptor alive could pull off. The veins, the shape of the nose, the imperfections in this woman's skin: impossible to capture.

Its eyes were simply gray globes, but Bree could swear it was looking at her.

She backed away and went down another step, almost falling from not looking at where she was putting her feet. She still wasn't convinced Irena wouldn't leap at her.

After almost tripping a second time, she risked walking down the stairs with her back to it.

She stopped again almost immediately, watching as a clay hand climbed the wall to the left of her.

It didn't seem to notice her, just slithering along, going toward one of the hives on the ceiling. Bree held her breath and stayed toward the opposite side of the stairs as she finished her descent.

The final distance was short, but the double doors were covered in a layer of clay. Not simply at the edges or forming an outline, but the whole structure.

It was well beyond what she could handle with a half-dried towel.

As she stood in front of them, mind racing as despair settled in, she heard a sound. Her pulse skyrocketed, and she spun around, looking for its source. The sound of Mr. Summer cracking echoed in her mind.

Nothing was moving. There wasn't even a hand crawling nearby her. But then she spotted a slight movement. Around a doorframe. The door to a supply room behind the reception desk. Human fingers eased it open. For a second: a bit of skin, a flash of hair.

"Wait … Bree?" someone whispered.

Bree instantly recognized the voice and stepped closer.

"Milda," she whispered back. "You're alive."

Milda opened the door slightly more. Her face was puffy and red with crying. She glanced around, gaze landing briefly on something behind the desk Bree couldn't see. Then she waved out her hand, gesturing her over.

Bree walked slowly. Out of the corner of her eye, a hand gently crept along, moving toward the floor.

She stepped around the desk and paused. The remains of a clay creature lay there. Its head was melted, and parts of its neck were a sludgy mess. Bree poked it once with the curtain rod, then stepped through the door.

Inside, there was only a single light, unadorned and hanging. The walls were mostly covered by shelves—some unadorned, some with filing boxes. It took a second for Bree's eyes to adjust as Milda closed the door behind her.

She was slightly surprised to see another person hiding. They had slightly sunburnt white skin and wore golden, square-framed glasses. A pair of simple dangle earrings matched their yellow shirt. They nodded at Bree.

"You killed it," Bree said simply.

"Haven did," Milda said, tilting her head toward the other person. "They were bringing me coffee … and threw it in the thing's face. It melted."

"They really don't like water," Bree said, holding up her barely damp towel. "I melted one in my room. Do either of you know … are people coming to help?"

Haven spoke up then. They were slightly shaking, breathing in short, shallow puffs. "The building was normal when I walked in; I don't know what it looks like outside. I'm not sure anyone knows this is happening."

"Fuck," Bree said. "The door is sealed."

Milda nodded. "Yeah, I looked away, and it was … it was like that."

"Do you know what happened?" Haven asked.

Bree opened her mouth, then spun to look at the door. The door handle looked so flimsy. So weak. She'd already seen that the monsters couldn't be stopped by a door.

"I think it has to do with the sky," Bree said, not looking away from the door. "You know that little girl?"

"What?" Haven asked. "What girl?"

Milda gasped. "Oh god, the little girl that kept asking for your help?"

Bree looked over her shoulder as Milda's eyes got wider. Bree gave a curt nod.

"I don't understand what you're talking about," Haven said.

"There's this little girl. She's been around the hotel since we all got here," Milda explained.

"And have you ever heard her name?" Bree asked, despite knowing in her gut the answer.

"No," Milda said. "I haven't."

"I think she's something else. An alien … or…"

"A demon," Milda said quietly.

"Yeah," Bree said, her shoulders drooping. "I think she changed everything. I'm not sure if getting out the door is the only way to survive this, but I don't think fighting the clay monsters is going to help."

"How is this happening…?" Haven asked more to themself than anyone else in the room. "This can't all be real."

No one responded, but Bree felt a drop in her stomach. The same she was sure the other two were having. Haven was right; this wasn't how the world was supposed to work. Monsters were from nightmares and stories.

"So, we need water?" Milda eventually asked.

"Yeah, that would help," Bree replied. "I think we'll need a lot of water to get through that door."

"Do you think the sprinkler system works?" Haven asked.

Bree's eyes widened. She'd not thought of that.

"The systems are really old," Milda said, "but they're required … so, yeah, they should still work."

Bree slowly reached down and opened the door a crack. She scanned around the reception area. After a few seconds, she spotted a shaped lump of clay on the wall. She'd been in the hotel long enough to know what was covered up by it.

She closed the door again and locked it. She turned back to look at the others. "The alarm's covered."

"So, we need water from somewhere else," Haven said, standing up. Their eyes narrowed in thought. "If we can get it wet again, do you think that towel's enough to unlock the door?"

Bree felt it over. "No, I don't think it can hold enough."

Milda bit her lip and then nodded to herself. "I've never been in the room, but there's a little service closet right over there. It probably has something connected to the sprinkler system we can trigger."

"That could work," Bree said, and moved to open the door.

A horrible sound started. It came from nearby. It was like nothing she'd ever heard before. Like what a person being deboned might sound like. A squelching, slimy sound with faint hisses.

"Oh god," Haven said.

Bree didn't even need to open the door to realize what was happening.

"They can get through doors. Run for it!"

She flung open the door and watched as a clay monster rose at the same time as a massive hole in one of the clay hornet's nests puckered shut. The monster sprinted directly toward the trio—moving as fast as the one that'd killed Mr. Summers.

The reception desk blocked it. The clay monster swept it out of the way in one move, shattering it into a pile of flying wood.

The trio screamed.

Bree whipped the towel at its head, knocking it as if she'd slapped it.

"Go, turn on the water," she shouted.

Out of the corner of her eye, she saw Haven and Milda scramble for the service door. The clay monster turned its head, seeming to consider changing targets. Bree whacked it in the head again.

The towel wasn't nearly wet enough anymore.

As it slid limply down its face, the monster caught it and pulled. Bree's hands burned as the rough fabric skidded out of her grasp. The monster loomed over her, and Bree could see darkness creeping into the edges of her vision. A soft whimpering escaped her mouth.

Bree gritted her teeth, screamed to force herself to move, and swung the curtain rod at the thing's head. The soft clay yielded immediately; the rod sliced into the side of the barely formed head. It didn't fall over, though—the clay coalesced around the pole.

And with the pole still there, the clay changed shape. Slowly forming a face.

Her face.

The fake version of her worked its jaw, and the curtain rod shattered. Bree let out a jagged cry and backed up. The only thing behind her was the small room. The dull yellow of the single bulb lit up her clay face. If she kept backing up, she'd be trapped inside.

She darted to the side, only for a tentacle of clay to smash into the wall. It punctured the plaster effortlessly. She skidded, moving to go the other way, only for multiple tentacles to lash in that direction, slicing just in front of her nose.

With nowhere to go, her gaze jumped to the approaching monster.

It loomed closer. A loose collection of gray mass. Bigger and bigger as it spread its form into long lines. A pair of legs topped by a mess of whipping tentacles. She took a single step back. A horrible pain crashed into her leg. She looked down on reflex as a tentacle crushed into her shin.

A tentacle ribcage like a mouth of teeth suddenly framed her, preventing her from moving anywhere. The faintest hint of sharp rib bones brushed her back.

Bree closed her eyes, hugging herself.

Bree hoped death didn't hurt as much as she imagined. She hoped that evolution had put in a gentle off-switch and that whatever came next would be all there was before she knew it.

The tentacle tightened its hold, and the jaw started closing. One of Bree's rib bones cracked on contact. The bone jerked sideways inside her. It was a wet fire, and she screamed hard as she drowned in it. She tilted her head back as fear became white bursts behind her eyes—

And then the rain came.

The sprinklers above her dropped buckets of water. Bree gasped in shock as awful-smelling, sludgy water left in the pipes too long coated the top of her head. She was barely aware of the lethal pressure stopping.

She opened her eyes. And let out one more shout. Her clay visage, so realistic, was melting in a shifting display of runny-egg eyes and collapsing skull. The mass of clay reached out to bite her, to crush her, only to slough away another chunk of itself.

She shoved it as hard as she could. It toppled backward on legs that were now mostly pillars of sludge. The clay monster looked like it might right itself for a second before its left leg broke and it collapsed. It writhed itself apart, melting into a puddle.

Even with the fire of her broken rib, injured fingers, and the awful smell of old, rotten sprinkler water, she cheered. The first joyous cry of this hellish day. She almost collapsed with relief as the wall's clay melted off in sheets everywhere she could see. The disembodied hands fell off their perches and splattered on the floor.

She leaned against the wall, trying to catch her breath. The front door was quickly clearing of clay. She watched with a weak smile as it sloughed off more and more of its covering.

The wall vibrated against her back. Bree stood up, moving away from it.

The rumbling quickly turned into sound.

The sound was ancient.

The sound that came from the walls, the ceiling, and even the air itself was petulant, modulated, and so full of an unearthly fury that something ancient in Bree's body immediately quivered in fear and warning. The part of her ancestry that feared animals bigger than humans, faster than humans, that knew what it meant to be prey, awoke and screamed in warning.

The clay by her shifted across the floor. Bree kept turning, glancing around in a panic. The clay of the whole hotel slid by some unknown force. Chunks shifted and exposed horrible things nestled inside. Hair mixed with brain pulp. Collapsed hearts crushed between rib cages. Snapped bones and marrow. It amassed in the center of the reception area.

It was so fast.

It formed like a reverse mudslide. Even with water slamming it down, it refused to melt. It grew taller and taller. A mound of clay and guts, with damaged eyes pockmarking it. Looking at her.

It radiated hatred so palpable that it made Bree's heart skip.

Chapter Ten

THE MASS OF CLAY AND BODIES FLAILED and smoked and seethed like it was boiling semi-liquid fat. Pieces of faces appeared on its huge surface. The eyes clustered into two giant globes. It bared a mouth of teeth in a myriad of conditions and levels of chipping. Noses crawled along its surface.

It became one impossible, huge, horrible face.

It roared again. The noise was so loud it made Bree clutch her ears.

A gasping, compressed sound came out of Bree's throat. Her legs were simply not working. The only instinct she could grasp onto was to hold still and hope the predator didn't notice her tiny form.

Tentacles waved in the air, and yet more ears, eyes, noses, and now tongues bubbled to the surface. Strands of hair swiveled from angry pores, vibrating in the open air like sea creatures on an ocean floor. A faint pulse moved along its surface until it was pulsing toward her—sliding as one mass.

Bree's shoulders tucked in; her arms went flat against her sides. With the greatest of efforts, she shuffled backward. Her heart rate had sped to the point she felt faint.

And someone took her hand. She resisted automatically, her body a stone she could barely control. But the pressure tugged, and she relented. She looked away, and it was like slicing a taut rope. A massive shudder came over her, but she got her legs to move again.

"Come on, come on!" yelled a voice.

Milda.

Bree found Haven tugging on Milda, who was tugging on her. They were still alive.

And now that she could move, Bree ran with all the energy she still had. She didn't so much travel as throw herself forward.

"The door!" Haven yelled and let go. Haven skidded to a stop and yanked on the handle.

And for a second, Bree was sure that it wouldn't open. Even with the clay removed. Even with all they'd managed, it wouldn't work.

But the door opened, spilling in the view of that horrible night sky.

The mass behind them screamed again. Bree's vision went wobbly, and she stumbled forward, almost falling. She didn't need to look back to know how close it was. She could smell it. Feel the energy rolling off it that told her how much it hated everything.

Milda collapsed to her knees in front of Bree, cowering and covering her ears. The cloying sensation in the air was coating each of Bree's breaths.

Haven ducked down, grabbed Milda's hand, and then Bree's. Haven moved jerkily, whimpering, but still pulled the trio to move again. The cool air was within reach.

Haven and Milda passed over the threshold.

Bree's legs stopped.

She looked down in disbelief. Her body was not working.

"Bree, come on!" Milda screamed. Her usual calm was gone. Her eyes were pleading, desperate.

Bree couldn't get her mouth to work.

A massive tentacle of clay and blood crashed into the wall. It sent plaster and water droplets flying in a pop of force.

Bree turned her head to look at it, and something yanked her from behind. For a second, Milda was still holding her hand. Then she wasn't anymore. Bree had let go without meaning to. Or perhaps because she couldn't hold on anymore.

The door swung itself closed. Milda and Haven screamed out, but their voices were instantly muffled. The solid wood severed the view of the outside.

Bree looked down at the huge wet mass curled around her stomach. A line of intestines ran through the clay encircling her, forming a vein. For a second, she simply stared at it in shocked silence.

Then a force like nothing she'd ever felt before pulled her back and off her feet. The air she would've used to scream disappeared, erupting from her mouth without sound. Her arms and legs shot out from the momentum.

The shuddering stop made her gasp. Then, with air back in her lungs, she let out a desperate, doomed scream. She pounded her hand against the tentacle and kept pounding even as a horrible sheen of pink blood-clay stuck to her arms.

"No, fucking no! *No*!"

A noise came from behind her: a dry sucking sound, followed by an echoing pop. Her heart sank as it occurred to her what was happening. The clay held her fast, and she couldn't even turn around—but she could picture the mouth opening. She felt the tentacle gently move her into something, something that's edges became all too easy to see as she was subsumed, and the escape closed.

An earthy smell washed over her, making her nose burn and her tongue feel coated.

Bree expected to die. The fire of survival had been doused too many times. She couldn't hope someone out there would save her—that anyone would be *able* to save her.

The tentacle gently spun her around and deposited her on the ground—a thick, sucking ground made of blood and clay. It pulsed like a heartbeat against her side.

And, for a few moments, nothing happened. Bree lay there. She breathed slowly. The pain of her rib and hands stung her mind. Bree kept her eyes closed, not sure why she was alive but wanting it to last.

So far, staying still was working.

But eventually, the pulse of the floor hurt too much, and her eyes drifted open slowly.

She wasn't happy with that choice.

It wasn't dark where she was. It was also too big. The mass hadn't even been two stories tall when it absorbed her; it shouldn't have been a cavern like this. But she stood in a rounded dome, lit softly pink and maroon. The ceiling stretched about eighty feet up, ending in a display that made her look back down.

It had only been for a second, but whereas most of the human remains she'd seen so far had been shredded and pulped, the man above was mostly intact. Nothing had been ripped off. The head was just not facing in the right direction. And very little was holding in his organs.

She breathed deeply to stop something erupting from her throat—a scream, vomit, something else—but the earthy tang was so thick. It tasted awful. She gagged on it, coughing. The sound echoed. After a moment, she stood up and spat on the ground. Her phlegm was pinkish.

The spot where her spit landed moved. No, the whole floor was moving. Something squirmed underneath the clay ground. A wobbling vein as wide as a snake traveled between Bree's feet. It stopped at the other end of the cavern, and a gurgle started. The gurgle was the wettest, stickiest sound she'd ever heard.

Bree reflexively backed away. There wasn't a lot of room in that direction. Right before she stepped into the wall of bloody clay, she stopped herself. Warning bells rang from the tips of her toes to the back of her eyes. She was certain that no matter what was slowly rising from that hole, it would kill her slower than if she let her entire back touch that wall. It was stomach acid. It was a bear trap. It was death.

She lurched forward as the floor sank. The clay sucked down, instantly encasing her feet. She tugged up hard, panicking. Bree even tried grabbing at her ankles, but they wouldn't budge.

The hole at the other side of the cavern widened further, and from that hole rose two clay men. Their faces were blank, formless, and slightly dripping. Each had what Bree realized was an exposed human heart suckered into their chests. They did not beat—they were damaged and wet and practically collapsed—but they sat where the heart should've been.

Bree whimpered in the back of her throat. This was it, surely.

The devil was arriving.

The clay men didn't seem to notice her. They faced each other, walked forward, and mashed into a contorted mass. It shuddered, growing lumps, then sucked them back in with sloshing sounds.

They formed a shape. Unclear at first. But it was a squat form with rounded sections. An oval backing and a flat platform.

It was a chair.

A throne.

The clay men's hands reappeared, sprouting like terrible plants, and grasped the ground with spindly fingers. A few odd settling motions made the throne wobble, but the hands eventually anchored it.

Bree held her breath. This felt like a ceremony. A show being put on for something's benefit. The chair now obscured the hole, but she was certain—certain down to her bones—that this was a chair for whatever was still down there.

Another horrendous, slick sound came from behind the throne. A series of growls and animalistic snarls happened next. The air stunk of ozone, then the cold copper of blood, then rancid oil.

The little girl walked around the chair. She was unharmed and without a spot of blood or clay. She hopped up slightly to sit on the throne.

When she opened her mouth, though, her voice was the entire cavern—it was booming, cracking, and too heavy.

"Hello, there."

She leaned forward in her chair.

"I told you that you had a chance to survive. Even your friends survived. You did a good job, Bree. Be proud of your accomplishments, even if I *could've* just covered *every* door in clay and slaughtered you all. But, again, that wouldn't have been very fair."

Bree couldn't think of what to say. Her mouth hung slightly open. All she could do was stare at this little girl who looked completely out of place.

Her hair was in a small braid now. Her posture, facial expressions, and eyes all looked human, childlike, and normal. She still had that smile missing a tooth. This really was the same little kid bothering her about making sculptures.

"You never told me your name," was Bree's eventual response.

"You always ask us about that."

Bree couldn't recall a single time she had asked that—but she wasn't going to correct her.

"I just wanted to know," Bree managed weakly.

The kid stared at her as if pondering a riddle. When Bree couldn't help but look back into her eyes, she finally saw something inhuman. Those eyes could witness travesties and inhumanity without shifting an inch.

"I don't have a name. Not a real one. That's not quite how this works. We sometimes make up one, but they're more like titles. We're a lot more than a name."

Bree didn't understand. She couldn't keep looking at that gaze.

"Are you going to kill me?"

The kid flicked up her wrist. The ground swelled briefly, and in a burst of motion that Bree had trouble parsing, another clay figure stood. Its posture was loose but fixed, like a store mannequin.

"No, you won. Last person alive in the hotel. And, besides, you taught me to make things in clay. That makes us friends."

"I taught you—"

Bree lurched. She couldn't stop seeing and hearing Mr. Summers dying. Recall him being squeezed until he bent and popped and broke.

The kid smirked and chuckled. It was a childlike sound. It was as if she knew what Bree had thought and found it enormously funny.

"You did teach me! I could've done all of this in an *infinite* number of ways with any victims I wanted. But I really did enjoy your choice."

The clay figure lurched to stand next to her throne. The little girl leaned over to it, lazily drawing lines with her finger.

"I see why you like it so much," the little girl said. "So malleable. So easy to work with. It's like drawing in three dimensions. Still quite limited, though."

The clay figure shrank. Its grayish skin turned various shades. Bree blinked and then jolted. Another Bree was standing there. Clothing perfect. Expression neutral. Height, weight, skin tone, all of it rendered as if a photo had been stretched into three-dimensional space.

"See, not bad, huh? Do you like it?"

"How did you..." Bree managed to say.

But she knew there wasn't an answer to that question. Not one she would understand. How had any of this been done? How had the world become strange, wrong, and dangerous? How had her own life been caught up in it?

The little girl clapped her hands. "It's not so hard when your air is more to our liking."

Bree tried to raise her foot. It was still stuck.

"It's perfect," the little girl said. "Look what it can do."

The child gently tapped on the fake Bree's temple. As if it was an on-switch, the copy of her lurched and twitched and then stood a little too straight.

"Are you going to kill me?" it asked.

Bree shrieked, covering her mouth.

"What a question, Bree! A very human question. And to answer … hmm. *This* version of you? Why, yes, I suppose I will."

With a light wave of her hand, Bree's clone shattered against the clay wall. It wasn't like momentum or a brutal hit. Her copy didn't fly off its feet. The clay body simply undid itself and splattered against the wall.

The inside of her clone was not loose clay. It was a duplication of her body—down to her brains, to her skull fragments. The chunks wetly slid down, then were absorbed into the floor's greater mass.

Bree couldn't take it anymore. A static sensation sparked up her back. She ran, even though she knew there was nowhere to run. But her legs were still stuck. The clay shackles gave only enough space, only reforming just enough to knock her off balance. She jerked and screamed and fell forward, twisting her ankle. That wasn't the worst pain, though. She landed flat on her stomach; her ribs were fire, lightning, and acid. Bree had even accidentally bit her tongue, filling her mouth with a faint copper taste.

She pushed up and spat out blood as it ran down her teeth. "Please, let me go. Or just kill me for real."

"Hmm. No. But enough playing around now, I suppose. We do have work to do."

"I won't do…"

Bree coughed hard. She stopped trying to speak. Her tongue hurt less when she didn't talk.

The little girl hopped down from her throne. "Oh boy. You're so fragile. I *always* forget. You'd think I'd know your species' strength with how many I squished today. I suppose we'll get a little better. Or stop caring."

As she got closer, a weight pinned down Bree. She felt something bigger than the cavern loom over her. Something with gravity all its own. She shrank away from it, pressure building in her eyes, teeth, and mind.

"I need you to help me with something very special, Bree. You spending time teaching me clay was wonderful, but it won't do enough. We can't make what we need with clay. We need so much more than that. More than you can give … but your soul will be an excellent starting point."

Bree spat out more blood.

"I would really prefer it if you agreed to this, Bree. It's so much nicer and cleaner if you feel like you have a choice."

"I would never choose … to … help…" Bree said.

It occurred to her that she could bite her tongue more. Try to drown in her own blood. Try to die before it did whatever it wanted with her soul. In this place, she was dead already.

Breathing hard, she moved her tongue out, resting her teeth above it. She didn't know how hard she would need to bite, but what was a little more pain?

The girl smiled at her. And her face was wrong again.

It was a mask. The girl's face was a mask. At the top of her eyes and the corners of her mouth, clay skin flaked away. Cracks spread. The forehead shifted slightly off center.

"Why, oh why, Bree, would you ever think death would help you?"

The child reached out a hand, and the hand was too long. At the shoulder and elbow joints, it was extending with new segments of gray clay. The presence, the pressure from before, exploded in Bree's mind. She couldn't feel her mouth or her tongue. She could barely perceive her own existence.

All that she was or could be was being pulled by an electric undertow. A force shredding and scraping at her essence.

When the clay child's finger touched Bree's temple, she was gone. Down, down deep. Into something static and spinning and twisting, like a roller coaster, but throwing her too hard, too fast, bashing her brains as it carried her to something below the entire universe.

The world faded, and a dream, constructed of such things that form dreams, nightmares, flights of fancy, and horrible persistent thoughts, descended on her mind. It was like crashing into a lake made of only the coldest, hardest, and most hateful water.

Chapter Eleven

SHE KNEW HER NAME. BRIANNA.

No, that wasn't right. She didn't like that name.

She liked what someone else always called her until she didn't talk to her very much at all.

Why did she stop calling her that? It was something sad.

Something that couldn't be undone.

Bree. Her name was Bree. She … made something.

Sculptures, that was it. There was a very tightly wound identity sticking to her, and it was someone who made sculptures. That was her personal identity, though. It wasn't what everyone else saw. No. No, that was something else.

Who was that face?

Oh, the mayor. Her dad. He'd been the mayor for how long? She couldn't recall when he hadn't been. Embarrassment? Surely that was the sensation she was feeling. Attached to those sour memories.

Why, though? What did he do?

Oh, right.

Helped make rent rise. Made people leave. Sold off whatever he could to mega-companies. Her school had all the funding. The public school couldn't even afford art classes anymore—couldn't afford so many things.

And her family was so rich with unearned money.

Was that the last time they'd talked? When they'd had an argument about a coffee shop. About his plan to raise the rent so high that a chain could come in.

No. It was about something else—

It was something about the sky.

Oh.

Oh, *fucking* god.

Where was she!?

Was she lying on the floor of that clay hell? Or had the little girl killed her like her double? Was she now in the real burning pit? Was the afterlife what she thought it was, and she'd been cast down?

Why didn't she have a heartbeat? What even was panic or fear without a body? She had the vague notion she should feel those emotions and that they could exist, but they didn't yet manifest.

Was this what being dead was like?

She couldn't see where she was. If she was dead, Bree expected a white void, darkness, Heaven, Hell, or something inconceivable to guess beforehand. But this was nothing. Not even the deep of space or a black hole. Just a failure to exist.

Except she was sitting on a bed, wasn't she?

Oh, maybe she was in … could be…

Things flickered into view as she expected to see them.

The door to her hotel room was there and uncovered in clay. She could see the bed she was sitting on. The room was as it had been. The door to the bathroom wasn't even broken.

There was the matter of the statue, though. She knew about it before she even looked at it. It sat in the corner of the room that didn't exist and tugged everything toward it. She eventually looked and was unsurprised.

Herself.

The statue was of Bree. Immobile this time. But it could conceivably move at any time. Nothing was off limits now.

The statue gave off a wrongness. A tainted pulse of air, full of that malevolent will from before. Like stale air and stale static.

Bree walked to the door instead. It glided effortlessly as she opened it. A gentle breeze met her. She felt maybe a diluted version of calm, then looked out the door.

Then the world was not calm.

It was rolling scales—like the surface of a reptilian creature, too big to see any more than a tiny section. The scales moved in and out toward her, a breathing, billowing motion. If she stepped out, she would fall onto that shiny surface and slide toward something unknowable.

Her hand tightened around the doorknob, finally feeling a muted version of what should've been fear. Even if she was dead, this thing was a threat.

The scales glimmered. In the intersections—the connecting point of plates—symbols formed. Symbols that could not exist. Outlines of impossible configurations. They meant words that could never be spoken. To pronounce them was to invite something horrible.

Bree's stomach jolted. She closed the door. Bree knew, deep down, that if she were not dead or dreaming or whatever was happening to her, what she'd seen would've obliterated her. It would've been the longest moment of her existence: years and decades and infinity, and then she would've been something new, something carved out and empty.

So, she closed the door.

Bree looked back into the room and failed to scream, cry, or express the emotions that should've been pouring from her mouth with such force they broke her insides. But to hold on to the thought of that thing outside the door long enough for such reactions was impossible. It simply wouldn't stay sharp in her mind.

Bree walked over to the bed and sat down. It seemed the only thing to do. The statue was still standing there, but she didn't look at it.

Instead, Bree looked at her hands. They weren't bandaged anymore, and the skin was angry, but she didn't feel any pain. She felt her sides, and the rib was in the wrong place, but didn't sting. Her tongue had the oddest indentation without the accompanying blood.

She looked back at the statue and thought about her life so far, or perhaps now, the totality of it. She thought about the statues *she'd* made for herself, for customers, for family. She'd spent the better part of each and every day for so long thinking of things she could make and how much people would love them. She could make a future. A legacy. A life where every day she woke up and did the thing she was meant to do, and then she would go to sleep and start again.

She'd make something that would outlive even this town.

Bree didn't know when the sadness started, but it did. That emotion was finally allowed to happen. Sitting there, unable to do anything, she felt sad. Bree was probably dead. Probably gone before her time.

Tears streaked down her cheeks.

She was kidding herself before, wasn't she? A legacy? How naïve. If the climate didn't kill everyone, then some politician would. A statue needs a base. And art needs a planet.

Her head tilted down. She touched her chin to her chest and cried harder. Maybe in death, she could admit how scared she really was about life. How uncertain she was of her future, every aspect.

She never grew thirsty. No hunger stopped her from weeping. Bree rarely cried, but when she did, she usually slept afterward. Crying was exhausting. But not this time. For an unknowable duration, she sat, anguished, and waited. Nothing happened. Tears came for as long as she could shed them.

The statue still looked at her.

"What do you want?" she asked it.

It did not answer.

Her statue looked so scared. Bree couldn't recall if it had before, but it did now. Her pupils were wide, and her mouth hung open in a scream.

Bree walked over. She reached out to touch the statue. Gently. On the shoulder. To see if it was cold like she would've expected before or warm as she expected now.

She didn't expect *pain*. The instant her fingers touched the clay, a horrible prick went deep into her skin. It was sharp and arching and made the hair on her arms rise.

She pulled back, sticking her finger in her mouth on instinct. It was still hurting. Everything else had been numb and cloudy since she'd returned to this room, but this pain was overly real. It was worse than it should've been. The body shuts down when faced with this kind of pain—except right now.

Once she was done gasping and wincing, she noticed she'd made a mark. Not on her skin, but on the statue. A dot the same size as her fingertip. Where had been clay was now the color of her pajama shirt—the same pink.

After a long moment of dread—and precision—she reached out and touched the exact same spot, avoiding even slight contact with the clay. It was warm. Warm in only the way a living thing could be. She'd been right—a person was trapped in there.

And she understood her hellish punishment.

She turned and went back to sit on the bed.

The wall was boring. The softness of the bed was muted, like everything else. She bounced her leg up and down for potentially years. She had no way of knowing.

She got off the bed and refused to look at the statue. Casting her gaze around the room for literally anything else, she went to the bathroom first.

Inside was a tiled room. It had no toilet, no shower, and no sink. The walls were spotless and boring.

Bree left the bathroom to look out the window. There was nothing beyond the window. Stars didn't come out in Quill Point anymore. They hadn't since the sky changed, but this view from the window was somehow worse. It looked like someone had taken a black cloth or piece of construction paper and covered the view from the outside.

She tried to open the window, and not only did it not want to open, but it was part of the wall. She looked closely, and the whole thing was fake. The frame was affixed to just a wall. The glass wasn't real; tapping it proved it was something like plastic or silicon.

Bree managed to muster some anger.

A tiny spark.

She punched the fake glass. It didn't hurt. Her hand dully bounced off it, numb and dry. She did it again—as hard as she could. If her hand or the window had been real, she would've broken one of them.

She started throwing punches incorrectly, tucking her thumb underneath her other fingers. One or the other—something would change.

She spewed swears. They came unbidden and automatically from her mouth. Over and over and over. At some point, she was begging. Then praying. Then swearing even louder.

Her hand was as it was. The window was fine.

She collapsed to the ground, leaning her head against the fake frame. Bree slowly, then with more assuredness, put the skin between her pointer and thumb into her mouth and bit as hard as she could.

Bree screamed. Her teeth would not cut. The skin would not break.

"Okay…" she said, slumping. "You win."

She slowly stood, her arms limp at her sides. Crying just felt like a waste of energy.

She placed her palm on the statue's face. Agony pierced her from every nerve to every synapse. Bree collapsed. She lay there, curled up, clutching her hand. Eventually, she uncurled, breathing hard despite seeming to not need the oxygen. She stood up.

Her copy was freed in a perfect handprint. One of her eyes was partially uncovered, and her mouth lay loose. She appeared to be asleep. Or in a coma.

Carefully, Bree reached out and gently tapped her copy's eyelid. The copy didn't react. The eyelid didn't even twitch. Bree tapped again. A small puff of air came out of her duplicate's nose.

"I hope you appreciate this," Bree said quietly.

She lifted her hand to free more of her, but stopped short. Surely, there was a better way to approach this. Some methodology that would maximize surface covered and minimize pain. She thought for a moment. It was like visualizing a sculpture before sculpting. Had she not been training all her life to think in those terms?

Eventually, she had an idea.

She gripped her arm with her other hand and extended a single finger. With a shaking that passed through her entire being, she ran her finger in a jagged line across the face. Then continued along her shoulders, then her side. She howled and screamed as she did. She traced line after line.

They were jagged and sloppy, but slowly she built a series of shapes that she hoped she could then peel off. She finished a clean loop, connecting two points, then let her hand drop. Her eyes rolled back, and she fell onto the bed.

A red haze was over her vision, and she had to lie down for a very long time. The pain didn't so much fade as get consumed by that numbness. That hollow feeling crept back in until it flattened her emotions and her senses.

She sat up and looked at her work. The lines weren't as random as she'd initially thought. They had a looping, curving, but still broadly geometric formation. It was like she'd made organic, fractal hexagons—that was the only way she could describe the pattern. And it was such a poor, *incomplete* way to describe them.

She leaned back to get a better look, and then suddenly whimpered. A desperate, panicked noise leaked out from her mouth. She scrambled back, her eyes going wide.

It had been an accident. She hadn't even noticed. The symbols on the copy's body were impossible things. They went beyond the confines of three-dimensional space. They were expanding and shrinking everything else around them.

She'd drawn the things she had seen outside the room. Underneath the miasma and sharp red of her pain, she'd been mimicking them. They'd gotten into her head.

She wanted to wipe them away, widen or blemish the design, but the symbols made it hard to pinpoint where the statue even stood in the room. The space around the symbols couldn't fit them. Bree reached out and instead touched the window. She swung her hand around wildly, and her fingers touched the linoleum of the bathroom.

When had she sat back down on the bed?

She kicked out, but her feet hit the front door. Bree stopped moving. The symbols crept along the walls, merging with the spaces behind and between them. The walls were the symbols; the floor was the symbols; the statue sputtered light as it expanded beyond her vision.

Bree moved to cover her eyes, but stopped when she raised her hands.

As everything around her warped and spun, all she could focus on was her fingers bleeding. Her fingertips were bright red. Blood traced down and pooled in her palms. They dried into symbols—crawling, endless symbols. They were flowing down her arm, up her palm.

She couldn't stop looking at them. They were everything. All was numb, anyway. Her pain. Her perceptions.

Her sense of motion or breathing or existing. These symbols were her future now.

How could she ever look away from what was destined?

Chapter Twelve

BREE AWOKE CLOUDY. HER MIND WAS sluggish and warm, and her eyes desperately didn't want to open. It wasn't too bright around her, but just bright enough in the way a sleeping person cannot allow. A brightness that, if fully acknowledged, would mean the day started.

But the damage was done, and her eyelids lifted. Though the more she met consciousness, the less pleasant it was. There was an ache across her. It also sat in specific places on her body, but she'd yet to perceive where they might be.

"You're awake," came a soft voice.

Bree stirred further, trying to place the sound. She cast her eyes around a simple room. A generic painting of a tree hung on the dull brown wall, and a television set was mounted to the side of it. It sat on a little swivel, displaying nothing.

"I..." Bree began, then stopped talking. Her throat was dry down to her chest.

"It's okay. The doctor said not to move much," the voice said again.

Bree dimly recognized it now. She turned her head gently.

Her blurry eyes met Milda and Haven. The pair were sitting in two high-armed chairs. Haven was apparently asleep. They lay with their head tilted backward in a position that looked slightly uncomfortable.

"Hi..." Bree said. She let the word linger for a moment. "Am I...?"

"You're in the hospital," Milda said. "We came back to get you."

Bree looked at her friend and tried to put meaning to those words. What had happened—something about clay and pain and red and strangeness—was all equally hazy.

Only that wasn't totally true. Something was pushing through her mind. Something was sitting beyond where she could perceive. A horrible ache made her stop looking at it too closely. She winced.

Milda moved forward in her chair. "Are you okay?"

"I'm ... just sore. What happened?"

Before Milda could answer, Haven made a small sound and stirred in their seat. Milda turned and gently tapped them on their shoulder.

"She's awake," Milda said.

"Oh, that's good," Haven muttered, their voice coming out in a tired whisper.

"They're always like this when they first wake up," Milda explained softly. A tiny and tired smile ran across her lips.

"Are you okay?" Haven asked, sitting up in their chair. "Are you feeling any better?"

Bree didn't answer at first. She really wasn't sure. The memories were coming in slowly. She recalled a horrible agony. A feeling of deep pain and shooting fire. Compared to that, this was better.

"I ... I think so. What happened to the hotel?"

Haven's face went completely pale. Even Milda's usually calm exterior disappeared, and she stared at nothing. Bree's stomach rolled, and a sharp pain came from somewhere in her body.

Haven eventually cleared their throat. "So, when you got ... taken. We tried to get back into the building. We really tried to open the door, but..."

Milda jumped in, her voice wavering slightly. "The whole outside was covered in that clay. And the sky was ... the clouds were doing something weird right above it."

"The sky..." Bree muttered.

She gently swiveled her head in the other direction, wondering if there was a window. There was. She wasn't sure if she was happy about that. The sky was still that horrible red and orange lattice. In the distance, the storm clouds let out faint lightning bolts, but no thunder.

She shivered, even though the blanket she was under was thick and warm.

"It was a nightmare. We had to get help," Milda said. Her voice had a tinge of apology. "We ran off to get someone—anyone we could."

"We found a police officer," Haven added. "But by the time we got back, the clay was gone. It was normal."

"Oh." Bree couldn't think of how to respond beyond that. "That's good."

"Can you remember what happened while you were in there?" Haven asked.

"I think she needs more time," Milda said, patting Haven on their arm. "It's okay, Bree. You don't have to talk about it."

"No, no, that's okay..." Bree said. "I'm just having trouble."

Bree ran her tongue over her teeth. Her tongue was also somehow sore. She couldn't remember why that would be. She was still chasing that elusive series of memories.

Another horrible stab of pain came from her body, and she made some attempt to find it. She moved around and finally noticed that her hands were heavy, encased in something.

She pulled one of her hands out from under the covers. The entirety of the skin was covered with a thick white bandage.

"It was all they had the tools to do," Milda said.

Bree remembered looking at her hands before. She remembered that she'd done something with them. It was *so* foggy. God, it was like looking through a stained-glass window. Bree's stomach rolled, but she managed not to gag. A horrible buzzing started at the back of her head. It would probably become a headache.

She slowly raised up her other hand. She couldn't remember why she was hurt. Her hand moved down to her stomach, where something uncomfortable was wrapped around her middle. Each time she took a breath, it hurt there a little.

"What happened to me?" she asked. Tears streamed down her face. "I can't remember."

"When we found you ... you were unconscious, surrounded by..." Milda sounded close to crying as well.

"*What happened...*" Bree whispered.

Haven looked back at her; their mouth tightened, and their eyes were full of some harrowing memory.

"Please tell me," Bree said weakly.

"We found you lying alone." Their voice caught for a second. "No, not alone. You were ... there were so many..."

Bree's heartbeat nearly skipped a beat. "Was anyone else alive?"

Haven just shook their head.

Milda gasped out a cry, almost shaking in her chair. Haven's gaze darted to her, and they wrapped her in a hug immediately. They pressed their forehead to the top of Milda's head. Milda kept sobbing but quieter, holding as tightly to Haven as she could—gripping their forearms and shuddering.

Bree watched this happen, but didn't quite *see* it. Her mind was flying backward, latching onto something like an anchor pulling a boat to a stop.

"Wasn't there a little girl...?" Bree muttered, and then the memories finally came to her.

It was like a waterfall broke free in her mind. A rush of memories held somewhere crashed down, spraying up thought after thought. She remembered how much it had hurt. She remembered—

"The symbols—"

Her entire body spasmed. She thrashed in her bed. Her mouth flew open, then shut so hard it left a ringing through her skull. Her head smacked into the pillow, and her neck stretched out.

Haven and Milda both jolted, breaking apart.

"I'll find a doctor?!" Haven yelled, getting up.

"I'm—"

Bree's mouth stopped. Her teeth did not move. Her entire frame was held loose and yet unmovable. She wanted to scream out something. To explain that there was something deeply wrong happening, more than they already knew. If the symbols were real, they were all in danger. They couldn't be allowed to—

"I'm fine," her mouth said suddenly, forcefully. "Please, don't worry, Haven. I'm sorry ... I think I went into shock, but it's over now. Did the doctors say what I needed to do?"

Haven stared at her. Their eyes were extremely wide.

"Are you sure...?" Milda asked.

"I think I should get someone," Haven said, moving slightly toward the door.

"No. No, I'm really fine. It was really scary, but it was all okay in the end." Bree's mouth forced itself into a smile. "I think I *would* like to talk to a doctor, but you don't have to go running for them. I'm sure my dad has one in specific I should get."

"I'll just find someone for now," Haven said. "Milda can stay here with you."

Milda nodded.

"Okay, fine, get someone. But you both go. I think I actually want a moment to myself," Bree's voice said. "I really would like just a moment to myself to think. Is that okay?"

Haven bit their lower lip. "Um, I don't think that's really a good idea..."

"Please, I just need a minute to compose myself."

Milda frowned. "Are you positive?"

"Yes, I'm really sure," Bree's mouth said. "Can you get me some food, too? Like some snack from the cafeteria, if they have any?"

Milda paused for a moment. "It's really not an issue for me to stay here. I can be quiet..."

Bree felt something horrible flow up her spine. It was rancid and tingling and hazy. It became her words, invisible and across the air.

"Thank you," her mouth said. "That's all."

Haven's eyes clouded over. Their usually alert gaze slipped down, and they slightly shuddered.

"Okay. Come on, Milda … let's give Bree a little space."

Milda's mouth drifted slowly shut. She glanced down and pursed her lips, moving her jaw like she was trying to open her mouth. After that didn't work, she frowned in confusion and stood up. She walked with Haven out of the room.

Bree wanted to scream for them to come back. That this was wrong—that something was extremely wrong. Her entire body was shuddering slightly against an invisible force.

But the door closed, and she was alone.

Only she wasn't alone.

Her head tilted to the empty chairs. She hadn't told her body to do that.

When she saw the little girl, she was allowed a small gasp.

The girl didn't look the same. Her skin and clothing were a dull gray color. The seams of her face mask were much more obvious now.

"Hello, Bree. You're doing such a good job," the little girl said.

Bree couldn't open her mouth, but the little girl nodded like she could hear what she was rather loudly thinking, screaming, pleading.

"I am sorry about you getting so beat up. Your species is so *fragile*. I just can't get over it."

Bree focused on just her arm. Maybe she could move a single part of herself if she really put effort into it. What she would *do* with her free arm, she had no idea. But it was *something*.

Nothing happened, though.

She tugged, and the muscles didn't even spasm or tighten.

The little girl tilted her head. "Oh. You want to move your arm. You only had to ask."

The girl waved out her arm, and Bree's mirrored the process. It was seamless, perfect, and not under her control. Worse, though, was the feeling that came along with it. She could feel the embrace of something along her back and coating her arm. She couldn't see the clay, but it felt like when the monster had almost crushed her. Only gentler, guided, pushing.

"I'm going to need a little more help from you, Bree. I need you to do me a few more favors."

Bree swore as loud as she could within her mind.

"I said you would get a chance to be immortal. I think all humans want that opportunity. Why make statues that will outlast you when you can help bring about something that will outlast *all* statues? I just need to borrow your body for a while—I'll even give it back—and you will be a part of something that will never, ever age. It's everything you ever wanted, no?"

The kid stood up, and Bree's body sat up in the bed. She turned her body, pushed out her legs, and planted them firmly on the ground.

"You won't have to worry about anything at all. We need a focal point in this reality, and you get that highest honor. You won't be harmed. You'll get to sleep and dream, even. We don't *have* to keep you awake. Did you like the dream I gave you before? I put a lot of thought into it. You can spend more time in your favorite hotel room."

Bree fought back against images of those symbols—those invading sights and vibrational fuzz that clouded her senses. The room was falling backward, with her in a longer and longer tunnel. The little girl's voice was getting harder to hear.

"This way, you're only complicit by inaction. By association. Your favorite."

The little girl looked less and less human. Taller. Stranger. And a laugh trailed and echoed down the tunnel—following Bree as she disappeared into herself.

She screamed in her head. Thrashed without motion. Her hands hurt, her body hurt, and her mind was sputtering, and she didn't even get the courtesy to know that she was asleep before it happened.

Bree's body remained upright. Bree blinked slowly a few times, then tilted her head one way, then the other. Her arm lifted up, then down. Bree's mouth formed a stolen smile.

"I wonder if he'll be mad if I start the summoning without him?"

Interlude Two

Town Meeting

THE MAYOR OF QUILL POINT. HE LIKED the title. He liked that he had earned it. Other people were citizens of Quill Point—people living in Quill Point. Constituents, staffers, and lobbyists. But there was only one him. Even if somewhere else there was another town named Quill Point, this town was his.

And having a town had its perks. While most people were now living cramped in the remaining houses or cold in sleeping bags around the bonfire, he had the ample space of the town's main governmental building. It was trivial to get his bed to it and place it in one of the rooms. He quickly discovered that he quite enjoyed sleeping next to where a judge would sit during court hearings.

Taking his coffee and walking through the halls was the ultimate morning. It was rejuvenating in a way that nothing else had matched.

Well, not *yet* could anything match it. But better things *were* possible, and there was always some new hill to climb.

As he sat and thought over the plans for tomorrow again, for the fifth time, The Mayor of Quill Point ran his hand over his desk. Another addition to the room. It had taken six boys to cart here. Solid oak, carved with laser precision. The hinges had only squeaked once, and his best men had gotten it perfect again. It cost the municipality a pretty penny, not that they knew it.

And it was worth every cent.

The fifth time thinking didn't yield new results. He looked at the clock and clicked his tongue. The waiting was annoying.

Now, The Mayor of Quill Point considered himself the perfect politician. He could support a bill that would make things worse for *almost* everyone and make it seem like an honest mistake. And then get reelected. He'd even somehow quelled—for a little longer—constant requests for at least the sick, injured, or young to stay in the government building. But his one fault—that even he had to admit—was that he was impatient. A long, long plan like this required utmost patience, but it made his jaw twitch. His pulse thumped in his chest as he looked at the clock again. His next meeting wasn't even late. It would be another fifteen minutes before that would be true.

But it was all he had left for today. Then he could relax in his bed for a few hours. Tomorrow, to begin with, he had to make it look like he wanted to bury the bodies.

The image of it alone made him chuckle. People going up to the Spire, to that which they couldn't *possibly* understand, and failing to move a person. It would be like a toddler claiming super strength and pushing a boulder.

Finally, after a few moments of moving papers around on his desk and considering a sixth mental run-through, a click came from down the hall—a person walking a little too quickly on old wooden boards.

The door opened, and a man with bags underneath each eye peered in. He was wearing a thick red jacket and had little lines of sweat dripping down his sickly pale forehead. He unbuttoned the jacket as he walked in, revealing a blue button-up shirt.

He managed to talk around mildly panting breaths.

"You called, sir?"

"Yes, please, come in and take a seat. We have some important matters to discuss regarding the current situation, and I'd like to get all the input from the town's most important and influential members. And, though I do wish for you to speak with some of our other experts, I felt it would be pertinent to discuss the matters at hand face-to-face."

George O'Conner blinked once, then nodded. He pushed up his large-frame glasses. The Mayor of Quill Point gestured at the chair in front of his desk, well aware it was slightly shorter than his own.

"Uh, yes, thank you," George said, pulling out the chair. He collapsed into it more than sat down.

"So, how have the recent attempts to ascertain the phenomena's origins gone?"

"Well, sir…"

George fidgeted in his chair. He tilted his head slightly back, meeting The Mayor's eye line. Almost immediately, his gaze flickered away again.

The Mayor of Quill Point smiled slightly. Nervous, as he had expected.

"Well, we've used what meteorological equipment we have, but it's not … we're not getting anything we can make heads or tails of if I'm being frank."

"I would prefer you be as frank as possible, George. We cannot have dishonestly at a time like this."

"Right, I ... I agree."

"So, is there *anything* we can find about this? If you can find a way to offer up something, anything, that might lead to a breakthrough, I can put in a request to reroute supplies to your team from the greater town. I'll accept a hunch, George."

"Well, uh, yes ... yes, about that..." George sputtered out for a moment, blowing out a little puff of air. "...I've seen what we have—the supply count and all that—and I'm not sure that would be wise. We'll start seeing complications soon as it is."

"The only way to free us is to have *you, or someone like you,* find a way, George." The Mayor clicked his tongue and leaned forward. "In fact, if you feel that a solo project is the best way to do this, I am entirely willing to reroute *most* of our resources to you."

George's eyebrows rose. He licked at his lips, thinking. The Mayor of Quill Point watched with interest. He looked for the twinges, the tells, and the moment a decision passed through George's mind.

"I feel like that would be irresponsible to everyone, sir. I can't take food from ... there are children, sir."

The Mayor nodded vigorously. "Oh, you're absolutely right. You're totally correct. I'm sorry about even suggesting such a methodology. To put all our eggs in any one basket would be foolish. I've been dealing with so much since—what are they calling it now?"

"Uh, Murder Sky, sir."

"Yes, Murder Sky. A tad ghoulish but not unwarranted. I've been dealing with the logistics of a town under siege. It must be getting to me. I've been having these spells of exhaustion. A little right now, actually. It's like election night all over again."

George's expression quickly switched to concern. He stood up from the chair. "Do you need me to get you a doctor?"

The Mayor of Quill Point shook his head and smiled. "That is appreciated, but no, no. I'm alright. We will get through this catastrophe, eventually. I believe in the strength, wit, and integrity of people like you, George. I've been interviewing plenty of people, seeing their perspectives on these matters, and the honor among you all has warmed my heart."

"Well, um, thank you, sir. Are you sure you're alright?"

"Yes, I'm fine for now. It shall pass. Thank you so much for your concern." He gave out the smile he practiced in the mirror. "And, even if I did need medical care, there's actually medical staff in the building right at this moment."

"There is?" George asked.

"Yes, actually, I meant to tell you more thoroughly. I alluded before that there are others here right now. And since you and I cannot find anything new to attack the 'Murder Sky,' I wonder if you would perhaps join a few others in a discussion. In the other room, I've gathered some of the best and the brightest of the town—the people whom I would expect to, if not utterly, at least contribute to solving the matter and would be best able to organize the town and the people. People with tornado experience, triage experience, those sorts of stellar members of our community."

He gestured to a solid wooden door a few feet beyond where they were sitting.

"There's a meeting going on *right now*?" George asked.

"Yes, they've been talking for about six hours now. You were the last person on the list of those I thought might be of assistance—it was organized not by merit; I meant no offense. I can't promise you will agree with what they've reached, but we need to be decisive in the next few days of this catastrophe."

George looked at the door but didn't move. He looked somehow even more tired. Strained out. With the orders The Mayor had been sending through the grapevine, he wasn't surprised. Staring at unknowable things with scientific equipment probably had that effect.

"I really do think the whole of the town could use your input on this matter," The Mayor added.

"Okay," George said, taking a calming breath. "I'll see what I can offer."

"Good man—a credit to our little town. I'd like to see a big city achieve this level of cohesion." The Mayor of Quill Point stood up and walked to the door. He smiled again.

George paused for a second more. Nervous energy, deep-bone anxiousness, was practically rolling off him. The Mayor could see in his eyes how much George's instincts screamed that something was wrong with this.

"Okay..." George said.

The Mayor of Quill Point opened the door and looked in. The room was slightly cramped because of the number of people sitting at a conference table.

"Hello," he said.

Twenty-three people looked back at him, all sweaty, all with some level of visual exhaustion. The coffee pot on a small counter, once full of decaf, was completely empty, and two grease-stained boxes sat next to it: the plain cheese no doubt devoured hours ago.

"Hello, sir," the chief of police, Tyler Peckham, said.

"Hello, everyone. I've got one more person to add to this conversation; I hope you do not mind. He's been studying what we can of the changing sky and might be able to help with this matter."

The subtle reactions were varied: some were dismissive, some angry. The head librarian, Felicity, gave him a suspicious look. A few of the community center employees—mostly those relatively fresh to Quill Point—actually seemed to still have hope of finding a consensus.

But The Mayor of Quill Point doubted there was *ever* a chance of that. If the order of people entering wasn't precisely tailored to stir conflict, they probably could've managed *something*, but grudges were excellent time wasters.

The Mayor turned and gestured George over the threshold. He slightly pushed on his back.

"George, please come in and talk with the others. He was just telling me how we may need to pool all our remaining resources to attend to the citizens and how we're morally obligated to put their comfort over a solution. Or something like that—he explained it better than me."

"That's not what I meant," George piped up.

"Oh, my apologies. As I said, I've been so tired from all of this. I leave the solution to this crisis in your capable hands."

"Um, well, I didn't mean—" George said.

"As I said, tell them, not me."

The Mayor of Quill Point closed the door, instantly silencing his reply. That room was soundproofed and had only one door in or out. He imagined a fresh argument was already growing.

He stood there for another moment, picturing the room. Checking off each name in his head. Were they all present, still? Was no one on a wayward bathroom visit?

Yes, all accounted for.

He crossed back over to his desk and sat down. He adjusted his sleeve, pulling back until a tight bracelet was visible. Attached to it, flush with his skin, was a small gold key. He slid the key off his arm and inserted it into the desk's hidden keyhole. Another reason the desk had cost so much.

The lock made the most satisfying click, and he swung open the compartment. Nestled snuggly was a wide black book. It was fine leather; only the edges were marred by its age. As books go, it wasn't the heaviest in the world, yet it still made a solid thud when The Mayor put it down on the top of the desk.

He gently flipped through the pages, careful with each turn. Inside were paragraphs of cursive and shoddy drawings in the margins. Some pages had scratched out things—words, images, or both now covered in a frantic lattice of lines.

The Mayor didn't dare dog-ear this book. Didn't dare mar it with a cheap bookmark. It took longer since it didn't even have page numbers, but he found the correct passage.

The cursive writing was so small, so frantic, but he read every line with deep familiarity. Some things were worth checking to be absolutely sure.

He nodded to himself. Yes.

All accounted for.

He stood back up and walked to the main hallway door. When he opened the door, there wasn't anyone nearby. When officers kept trying to talk to the police chief, he'd sent them to oversee the bonfire for the night.

"Are you around?" he yelled, cupping his mouth in his hands. "Are you here?"

As soon as the words finished echoing, the lights turned out in a wave of darkness.

A giggle came from within that dark. High-pitched. Then the sound happened again and got sharper. The giggle became almost a joyous scream, like people zipping by on a rollercoaster.

A pair of glowing yellow eyes opened at the very end of the hallway. They were close to the ground but too large for the small, barely visible figure.

"They're ready for you," The Mayor of Quill Point said.

The hallway got darker. Cave dark. Pitch black. And the yellow eyes shimmered and then jolted in zig-zag lines—flowing from wall to ceiling to wall down the hallway.

The giggle turned to a wet snarl.

The Mayor of Quill Point stepped backward into the room, and the door slammed closed in front of him.

After a second, there was a calm knock.

The Mayor opened the door and bowed to the small boy standing there.

The boy smiled with a grin missing a tooth.

"Hello, Mayor of Quill Point."

"Hello. It is my honor to be in your presence. I truly cannot thank you enough for gracing me with a visit."

The little boy giggled and walked around him. Instead of going to the room, he went to the desk. With a hop that got a little too much vertical distance for a normal person, he landed on the edge.

He picked up the book and flipped through the pages.

The Mayor said nothing, just watched.

The little boy stopped on a page and stuck out his tongue. Then he placed it back down on the desk. When he looked at The Mayor again, his eyes briefly glowed yellow.

"Are you sure that's everyone? All those little bugs are in the right place?"

"Yes, I made sure of it." The Mayor bowed his head slightly.

"Good. My sister is done goofing off, and we're done being nice."

Fear bloomed in The Mayor's chest. "Oh, has she chosen...?"

The boy giggled again and pointed at him. "Oh, look at you, worried about a bug. Why does it matter? But, yes, your daughter won. She'll be spared."

The Mayor of Quill Point couldn't help but feel a surge of relief. He smiled. "Thank you so much for honoring my family by serving you."

"You talk way too much," the boy said.

He hopped down from the desk; the landing was much heavier than it should have been. Each subsequent step had a gravity, a pull that made loose papers shift and furniture skid slightly.

The Mayor of Quill Point gestured to the door with another bow.

The little boy's face looked wrong as he approached. Pure black smoke came from around the edges, from around the mask that made him look like a human child. It leaked from his tear ducts, from the corners of his smile.

"Don't open this door until I am done," the little boy said.

The Mayor simply nodded.

"Good little bug."

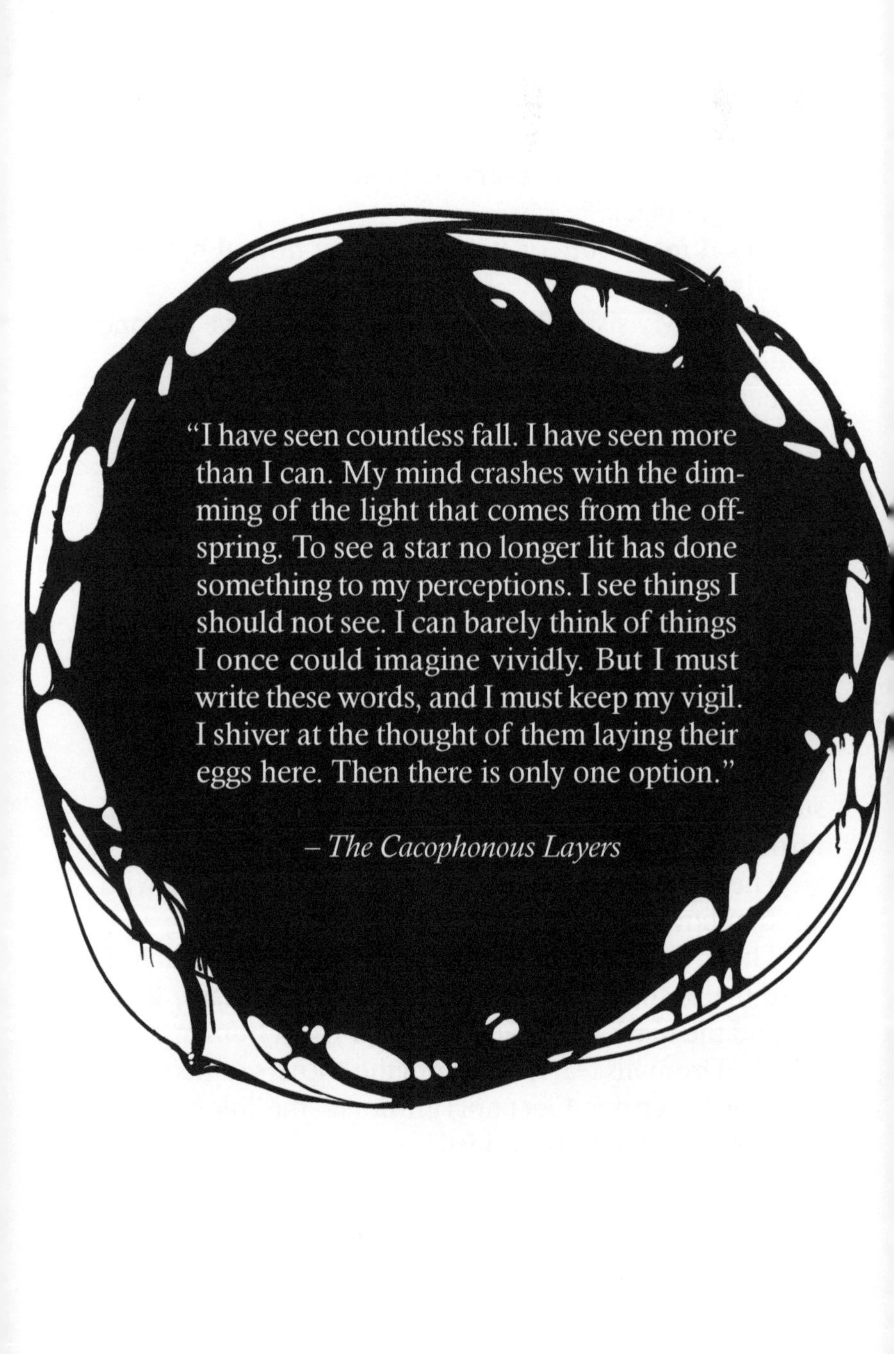
"I have seen countless fall. I have seen more than I can. My mind crashes with the dimming of the light that comes from the offspring. To see a star no longer lit has done something to my perceptions. I see things I should not see. I can barely think of things I once could imagine vividly. But I must write these words, and I must keep my vigil. I shiver at the thought of them laying their eggs here. Then there is only one option."
– *The Cacophonous Layers*

Part 3

Emptied-Out People

Chapter Thirteen

Caleb lay in a dark hospital room. He hadn't slept. How could he sleep? He'd done nothing all day but lay in this bed and wait for the hospital to kick him out. The only thing going was his mind. That racing feeling that came more and more lately.

His stomach felt off, but he wasn't hungry. He'd eaten—but the food was terrible. Cold porridge, reheated bacon, and burned coffee. All the fresh food in the town had spoiled.

He let out a sigh and rolled as best he could. A wrong motion made his lower back twinge. He tensed, lying half on his side, gravity tugging at him. Caleb let himself fall back on his back, accepting the discomfort and his insomnia.

He reached over to his phone on the small bedside table. The internet was gone, but his photo application still worked. He wished it didn't.

A picture of his student loan agreement signed and damning. A "For Sale" sign so excitedly and optimistically recorded when first moving to Quill Point. A view of his ex-girlfriend, Sarah, standing next to him while smirking and holding up a pair of sunglasses. He tried not to look at himself in the picture. He'd managed a decent tan on his beige complexion for a while, but he still hadn't gotten shaving right back then. And he absolutely hated how his blond hair sat in that awful, self-made haircut. Though he also didn't much like the itchy mini-beard and close-cropped style he had now.

Next came the calculations, as inarguable as gravity. He couldn't just look at the pictures, no. The worry was a fist around his brain.

They said no one was charging. That he could stay until they were sure he was fine, free of charge. Nothing for the food, nothing for the care, nothing for the bed, and it was *bullshit*. Everything costs money. Even time. *Especially* time.

Caleb counted out what his hospital bill and loan interest would become once Quill Point met the world again. He didn't even have insurance.

Sleep would probably help stave off panic. The problem with sleep is that it requires a lack of thinking. The problem with not thinking is that it's difficult to not think about not thinking. The problem with panic is that once you realize you're panicking, you're thinking about panicking, and it's hard to stop panicking when thinking about—

He pulled up the calculator app. Tried a calculation. No good. He was screwed. Interest rate. Debt. Forever. How about—

Nope. The numbers don't lie.

Caleb turned his head toward the orange pulse. The one he could see even from the hospital. The bonfire for most people of the town. Most houses weren't livable anymore. Not since the sky—

Oh god. The sky. The earthquakes, and the hands, and the corpses—

Caleb tried to time his rapid breathing to the embers, to the slower, steadier rate of a raging fire. Slow down his heart—

Caleb dropped his phone. It slammed into his chest. And it was going to burst. Was that possible? Could it explode like that?

"Hey!"

Caleb jolted. He sat up as a small bedside lamp turned on. The yellow light made his eyes hurt.

"Breathe. You're okay. Hey, hey, breathe now."

Caleb looked wide-eyed at his hospital roommate. Caleb's entire form was shaking, but some part of him still perceived his friend.

Gabriel held up his hands and breathed slowly. He held Caleb's eye line and bopped his head gently. It took several moments of matching Gabriel's breathing, but Caleb's racing mind slowed.

"You're okay," Gabriel continued. "It's okay."

"I was... I was..." It was hard for Caleb to get it out. His mouth kept moving to speak, and then no words escaped.

"Breathe."

That instruction made sense. He over-committed to the action, sucking in so hard he coughed. That awful food rose to his throat like it wanted freedom.

"I'm sorry... I'm sorry—" Caleb sputtered out, lungs officially hurting. He coughed again, then finally sucked in a good amount of air.

His eyes burned. Caleb was sure he would cry any second now. How could he feel so tired and yet so wired simultaneously?

"I'm so sorry," he said.

"It's okay," Gabriel said. "Are you okay?"

Caleb didn't answer for a long moment. He felt twitchy, but the overwhelming flood was receding. He put his hand on his chest, and his heart was still working.

"I was just … worrying."

"I thought so."

"It's just…"

Caleb frowned.

How do you put into words that you're pretty sure your financial future is obliterated?

"I'm worried about what's going to happen after I can't stay in the hospital anymore," Caleb eventually said.

Gabriel pursed his lips. Gabriel had lightly tanned white skin, long blond hair, and deep crow's feet behind his thick-rimmed glasses. Only partially visible underneath his black shirt was a bandage for his collarbone. He'd somehow also burned his left hand long ago, and when thinking hard, he'd scratch at the long, red scar.

"I don't know. I don't know at all. But it'll be okay."

"You don't know that!" Caleb shot back. His voice came across harsher than he meant it to. "It's all going to burn—"

"Hey, hey, stop," Gabriel said, his voice going soft again. "It's not going to burn."

Caleb shut his mouth hard. The accusing words wanted out, but he held them there. "Okay."

"Okay?"

Caleb nodded.

Gabriel stared at him for a long time. He looked exhausted. Like it was only his willpower holding open his eyes. Caleb had noticed him pulling several all-nighters this last week studying.

"You should try to sleep," Gabriel said. "I can get a nurse to bring you something."

Caleb considered it. He hated the way sleeping pills made him feel afterward. Underneath the blanket, his toes tensed and relaxed as he tried to get his mind under control.

"No… I'm okay."

"You're sure?" Gabriel sounded dubious. "You really could use the rest."

Caleb nodded and laid his head down, tilting his chin so he could still see Gabriel. "Thank you for helping me."

"Oh, of course." Gabriel had the beginnings of a smile. "It's what I do."

"I know. I'm okay. Really. I just… it gets bad."

"I understand," Gabriel said. "Are you sure you don't need… we can talk if you need to?"

Those last words came out slightly mumbled, loose with exhaustion.

"No, no. It's… I'll be okay until morning."

"Okay…"

The light flickered off, leaving only the orange glow to pierce the room again.

"Goodnight, Caleb. Seriously, I'm here if you need me."

Caleb didn't answer. Guilt was his newest horrible sensation, and it was thornier and heavier than panic.

He lay there, staring at the inside of his eyelids. He felt so tired, just not in the way in which he could sleep. More like his chest was an open, yawning mouth and his stomach a clenched muscle.

An hour passed, and his eyes burned. There wasn't even a clock in the room to tick. Gabriel's eventual soft snores became the only sound except for Caleb's heartbeat. That was comforting.

It wasn't enough. His eyes snapped open.

The bed had become even more unbearable. It was a flat sheet. It wasn't touching the floor, but he could swear he felt the grout rubbing against his back. The mattress had petrified somehow.

He slammed his eyes shut again and *willed* himself to sleep. To go unconscious. Screamed it internally. Willed it like a wish. But he wasn't even that lucky. There was only one option. He wouldn't wake up Gabriel again.

Caleb had no clue how to do this quietly enough. He tugged the blanket off himself slowly, waiting for any change in Gabriel's breathing. After another moment, he slowly sat up in bed.

His entire body yelled at him for doing so. Somehow, the telephone pole had only broken a good chunk of his studio apartment and none of his bones—but it left him completely sore. The painkillers they had left were not doing it for him.

The problem with not sleeping was becoming apparent. He was wobbly. Little pants came out unbidden as he crossed the relatively small room. He looked back once, peering over the stack of medical textbooks to Gabriel's sleeping form. Another stab of icy guilt. This town *needed* him as soon as he healed and waking him up was not helping with that.

Caleb pursed his lips and fought back tears. Eventually, his shoulders fell, semi-relaxed. Then he turned around and silently made it to the door.

Strictly speaking, Caleb wasn't supposed to wander the hallways even during the day, but he had a feeling no one would care. In a short-staffed hospital, with medical supplies running out and little clean water, his late-night walk wasn't worth anyone's radar.

He closed the door behind him with a slight rush of air. The silence in the hallway was broader, more acoustic. Like each non-sound stretched its limbs down the hallway. It was a tunnel of linoleum, with mid-height blue lines on both walls and dimmed overhead lights. Almost above his eye line sat a large picture of Irena Ink. She looked down at Caleb with a stoic expression. His tired brain made the picture seem like its eyes were shifting and the shadows around the frame were moving. Almost like reaching fingers. Like the hands that pulled people screaming into the sky—

The panic surged again. A fire that might eat his lungs. His hand curled into a fist. His knuckles turned pale white. A long minute passed, and he slumped again, breathing even harder. He wished he could go a day without feeling like this. Everyone else glided through life like it was easy to talk to strangers, be productive, be logical, and then act logically. They acted like the weight of things was possible not to feel.

Caleb swallowed back tears and walked again. Trying to think about anything other than what he was currently thinking about. The simple sterilization of a quiet hospital didn't offer many distractions.

He paused as he passed a particular door. The hospital was not large—but he still marveled that the mayor had let his daughter be anywhere near ordinary people. She was the royalty of the town. But something supernatural had happened in the hotel she'd been staying at. And now she was here. And people were dead. Lots more people. That's all he'd heard about it.

That's all he wanted to hear about it. That's all he'd let people tell him about it.

But it being her room wasn't the only reason he stopped. It was also because the door was open, and the bed inside was clearly empty.

He wondered if she couldn't sleep, like him.

Caleb pursed his lips, thinking whether he wanted to run into her. Brianna was not someone you pissed off. He couldn't go back to the room, so there wasn't much choice, but he'd probably turn the other way if he saw her.

Keeping this in mind, Caleb set a course for the empty cafeteria. He'd seen people deliver food to her room, so it was doubtful she'd go there. And he might find something. Something comforting—perhaps he should try tea.

The remaining walk wasn't long, but his back was slick with sweat as he rounded the second corner. Lying in bed and healing had made everything exhausting. He used to pull double shifts at the Ink Well Diner, but he was out of practice.

He found someone looking back at him when he opened the double door, sitting in the semi-dark. A jolt of fear hit Caleb, but he recognized who it was.

"You're up," James said, his voice sluggish. He tilted his head, letting his already deteriorating man bun fall apart. "Also, you're not supposed to be out of your room."

"Y-yeah, I just needed some air," Caleb replied. "I can go back—if you need—"

James shrugged. "It's whatever. It literally doesn't matter."

"Oh, okay," Caleb said, relaxing slightly and managing a smile.

"Not much to do but be awake," James said, gesturing at a cheap white cup.

James had gentle brown eyes and laugh lines. But those eyes were bloodshot, and he had premature gray hairs and too many wrinkles on his light brown face. He stared down into his cup as Caleb moved into the room.

"Why are you up?"

"I was just worried..." Caleb eventually said.

"Aren't we all?" James replied flatly. "Come on, sit down."

Caleb nodded, sitting in one of the uncomfortable bucket chairs. It skidded against the linoleum, and the sound seemed to bounce around the room. James just quietly looked in his general direction but never directly at him.

"I was worried about what would happen next," Caleb said.

Even as he said it, he knew how unhelpful a statement it was. But he felt compelled to keep talking about it, verbalizing it, running the tape repeatedly that played in his head.

"Yeah, like I said, join the club," James replied.

He took a long sip of the coffee. After a moment, he looked down at what Caleb assumed was an empty cup and sighed. It was a sigh so full of disappointment that Caleb couldn't help but feel it was aimed at him.

"So much college, nursing school, a debt you would not believe. All for people vomiting on me, and then the world ends. Talk about helping people." James swirled the empty cup like it was a wine glass. "That's what I think about. Maybe you can top it. What about you? What's keeping you awake?"

Caleb sat there, feeling increasingly awkward. How could he complain after a statement like that? But James kept staring at him like he wanted an answer.

"It's just… it's all going bad." Caleb frowned to himself, the words looping in his chest, echoing with each utterance. "I just… I k-keep looking at the sky, at the town, and it all seems so b-bad. I don't know how it will ever get better. Once I'm out of here, they're going to charge me. I just know it…"

Caleb wanted to puke.

James breathed gently through his nose. He delivered his following sentence without sarcasm, dry as a twig. "Do you know what it's like to see someone die?"

Caleb flinched in his seat. He shook his head.

James looked down into his cup. "I had a patient die on me today. His body failed. I know why it happened medically—we ran out of heart medication—but I don't know why it happens. It makes it so I can't sleep, though. Dead people look like they're sleeping."

James leaned his head on his free hand. His eyelids dipped like he was falling asleep, but his voice stayed the same. "I get the worrying. It doesn't help. But nothing does. It didn't help that man. And right now, people will die if we do anything. It's fucked, my guy."

He splayed out his hands, chuckling. It sounded wrong, his mouth not moving right. The noise was like it was recorded in another room.

"I'll probably die soon too. We've only got so much insulin in this fucking town."

James didn't notice how long Caleb sat and just looked at him.

"Uh… um, are you…?"

James stood up suddenly, not seeming to hear him. He walked to a dingy coffee pot. Caleb watched James slowly, mechanically, go through the motions of filling a cup, adding milk, and pouring sugar packets into it at such a high quantity it raised the liquid level above the cup's lip.

He looked at the puddle.

James walked back toward Caleb and sat down silently. Another moment passed, and he sighed.

"You're the second person I've said that story to," James said.

"Okay…?"

"Some girl was wandering the halls. The mayor's daughter. She asked."

"Are you okay?" Caleb replied. His concern was doing a decent job of overpowering the awful feelings in his chest.

"I'm not," James said like he answered a math question. "I'm really not. But I don't care. Nothing to do about it, anyway."

"Can I help you?" Caleb asked.

"No," he said. "But you don't need to help me. I like the silence. It feels less like this is all a long, long nightmare."

"You should, uh, you s-should get some sleep," Caleb stammered out, realizing how hypocritical that sounded.

"I'm the only nurse here right now. I don't know where the rest went. They should come back in the morning, maybe. If a patient needs me, I have to be there. I don't get to sleep. It doesn't matter how I feel."

He cast his tired eyes at Caleb, and his jaw barely moved when he spoke.

"Sleep for me, won't you, Caleb? Dream for me."

Caleb couldn't help but nod. He wanted to run away. Those words had made something in him twitch and a warning bell toll.

He got up for the door. He'd been hungry, but now even that sensation didn't fit.

Caleb glanced back once, and James hadn't moved. His hand was wrapped around the coffee cup like it was part of his skin. The coffee looked cloudy under the poor light. The cafeteria's silence had rapidly become so distinct and weighted that Caleb couldn't bring himself to say anything more.

Caleb briefly wondered if this was a dream. The world had rapidly become surreal. The way people talked about recent events felt staged, fake, like a joke where the punchline never came—a prank on an entire town.

He almost wished it was a dream, even if it was a nightmare. He lost his home, and maybe that could be a dream. Another person was falling apart before him; perhaps *that* was a dream. People had died in horrible, fucked-up ways; maybe that could be a dream.

He let the door close behind him, leaving James like he didn't exist, and walked back the way he came. The path felt quicker. Like he was floating. Like his stress was borrowed from someone else, and they were taking it back. The warning bells slowed, dimmed, and he finally got the right kind of tired. Heaviness descended on his brain.

When he entered his room again, Gabriel was thankfully still asleep. He was breathing softly, a blanket covering all but the top of his head.

Caleb's tiredness pressed harder on his skull, making him pant from holding himself up. He nearly toppled multiple times. Curiosity, worry, willpower, everything quickly succumbed to that dizzy tiredness, and where his bed had felt awful before, it now was the most luxurious thing he'd ever touched. Unconsciousness came wholly and rapidly.

CHAPTER FOURTEEN

GABRIEL ALWAYS WOKE UP CALEB somehow. Whether it was just the rustle of a medical textbook's pages, his muttering of notes, or eating his breakfast a little too aggressively, Caleb always shot out into the world against his wishes.

So, with great confusion, he woke up feeling refreshed. Caleb opened his eyes to the streams of sunlight coming through the strange tendril sky. He muttered to himself before sitting up in bed.

He jolted slightly when he noticed that James was sitting next to Gabriel's bed, staring at him. It didn't look like James had gotten any sleep—the bags underneath his eyes had gotten somehow more pronounced. Gabriel seemed to have had a similarly bad night. The blanket was barely covering him, his arms and legs sticking out from under the covers. His blond hair was a mess, snarled into multiple tangles.

Caleb waited a moment, watching James continue to stare. It wasn't clear James was even breathing.

"Uh…?"

James raised a finger to his lips, not looking away. Caleb opened and closed his mouth silently. He glanced out the window. It could be as late as noon.

Caleb tried to keep his voice low. "What's going on?"

James shook his head, then whispered, "He needs to rest up for it."

Caleb nodded automatically. Then thought about it.

"Rest up for what?" Caleb asked.

James swiveled his head. He was still not blinking. His mouth moved like it was being swung along a hinge.

"His surgery, of course."

Gabriel muttered and groaned.

"Now look what you did," James said, not a smidge of actual chastisement in his voice. "Oh well, may as well begin."

Gabriel groaned again, and James leaned over him, pushing at his stomach with a rhythm like he was kick-starting a stopped heart.

"Come on, wake up," James said.

"Uh, that seems like a bad—" Caleb began, but stopped when Gabriel shifted.

Gabriel rubbed at his eyes for a few seconds, then rose to sit. Drool stuck his thin facial hair to the corner of his mouth, and his eyes weren't fully open.

He looked beyond wiped out. He looked like he was resurrected from death, and something hadn't come back fully. Like there wasn't a soul behind those eyes.

He let out a wet groan deep within his throat and cocked his head. "What is it?"

"It's almost time," James informed him.

"Oh. Oh, wonderful."

"What surgery are you talking about…?" Caleb asked.

James chuckled flatly. "It's not time for you to know."

"It's necessary, though," Gabriel added. "The only thing necessary. Nothing else matters anymore."

By this time, Caleb understood. He wished he didn't and wished it would stop, but he'd seen or heard of too many paranormal things in the last while not to notice it when it was happening. But he didn't know what to do.

All he knew was the two people in front of him were not acting like the two people he'd known.

"What about..." he grasped at something normal to ask. "What about the stuff you're studying?"

"Oh, yes, that. Pointless. I don't want to do that any-more. I want to stagnate."

"*Stagnate*?" Caleb replied. "Is that ... is that a medical term for something?"

"No, it's not," Gabriel said.

James nodded along in agreement.

"I mean rot, dissolve," Gabriel continued, "become nothing. The mud, then carbon, then nothing. It doesn't matter. It never mattered."

Caleb felt like things were spinning. Like the world was without a center of gravity or an anchor. Panic was squeezing at the sides of Caleb's skull. His throat felt like it was closing.

"W-what doesn't m-matter?"

Gabriel's head lilted to the side. He caught it with the palm of his hand. If he hadn't, he would've toppled right off the bed.

Instead of answering, Gabriel replied, "Did I ever tell you what happened to my brother?"

Caleb slowly shook his head. "You j-just said he passed... passed away."

Caleb's eyes darted to the door. Could he run away? Should he try? Would he even make it halfway before they did whatever they were going to do?

"He did," Gabriel responded. "He died when I was a little kid. He got hurt on the swings. Someone wasn't maintaining the equipment. Something about not enough school funding: it broke while he was on it. It was like slow motion."

His entire body swung the other way, only caught by his hand hitting the mattress at the last second. It reminded Caleb of a doll slumping on a shelf.

"The metal came apart when he was at the top of an arc. It collapsed around him. I was running to help him, yelling for our mom."

He leaned forward, mouth barely held closed. A smell was coming from him. Something metallic and pungent. "The fall itself didn't hurt him much, and I pulled him out quickly. But the metal cut his arm. A long, horrible gash. It was so sharp."

Caleb's gaze dropped to Gabriel's hand. And he wondered if that scar was really from a burn.

"Wrist to the elbow. You could see bone."

Caleb's heart was hammering. His lips were so dry they were sticking together.

"D-did he die of … blood… blood loss?"

Gabriel held him in a silent look for too long, then shifted himself back so his head was almost tilted to look at the ceiling.

"No. We got him bandaged up and stopped him from crying. He died because we didn't have insurance, and we couldn't afford to see a doctor a second time. And it looked like a regular fever. Then he died."

Caleb was crying. In fear, sadness, and this awful spinning feeling still growing in his stomach. He wanted to scream at … *something. Anything*. If it would stop this. It was like listening to a politician describe a death toll.

"Death happens like that," James quietly commented.

The spinning sensation got even worse. Caleb clutched at his head. These feelings were well beyond what he usually felt, even during the worst times. The edges of his vision had a pulse to them, and it *wasn't* coming from inside his body or mind—something was pushing hard on the boundaries of…

He didn't know what exactly.

But he could swear the distant sound of breaking glass was crackling through the air.

Gabriel didn't seem to notice his distress. James simply nodded at it.

The words Gabriel spoke next rolled like a boulder—without thought or consideration.

"That's why I became a medical student. If I had known anything I do now, I could've helped. Or at least warned someone. My mom was dealing with three kids and no husband. That rich fuck never paid child support. But if a doctor could've lived in our house, my brother probably wouldn't have died."

Gabriel delivered his next words with a shrug.

"But people die all the time. What makes it special that one of them was related to me? Every car crash is someone's child."

He shrugged again, then looked over at James.

"I'm ready for the surgery."

Two men entered the room as if they'd been waiting for a signal. Caleb's gaze snapped to them. They were wrong. The surrounding air was wrong; the sensation of being in the same room as them was oily.

They weren't human.

They were extremely pale, tall, thin, in scrubs—*no*, a suit. It depended on when he was looking at them. Blood-slick, ripped-up scrubs. The fanciest suits he'd ever seen. Watches that cost more than anything he'd ever owned. Latex gloves coated in bile.

And their faces blurred. It was a ruined photo in real life, a dream-logic half-memory. They had the idea of a male face with nothing to hold on to, nothing to remember.

Caleb rubbed at his eyes. They burned. The air was so slick and coating and rancid.

The two men moved fast. Caleb wasn't sure their feet touched the ground as often as they should've to get across the room. But then they were on either side of Gabriel. Something unseen pushed James out of the way.

Caleb knew they were smiling down at Gabriel. And couldn't tell where the idea had come from. It was impossible to see any expression on their faces.

"Uh, no, but ... wait..." Caleb said. It was increasingly hard to think straight. "W-when did this happen?"

"Knowing I wanted to stagnate?" Gabriel asked. "Oh, very recently."

The two men silently helped him stand, holding him by his armpits.

"You didn't tell me about it..."

"Oh," Gabriel replied. "Well, it's just what I need to do. There's no other option."

"*It's simply the state of things.*"

Caleb's back straightened. A cold sweat washed over him in a second. One man had spoken. Only he hadn't. Neither had moved their mouths. The voice was in his head.

"*It's how it is.*"

That was the other voice. Caleb could tell because it was in a slightly different pitch.

Gabriel walked with them as they glided across the floor. They were at the door before Caleb could even think of what to do, and its closing clang made him softly scream in the back of his throat.

James sat down across from him, staring with the same flat expression as last night. "I know this is scary for you, but it'll be okay. You're just not seeing the big picture."

Part of Caleb wanted to scream—part of him wanted to hit James in the head. His panic was becoming something else, and he needed to… he *needed* to stop this.

Whatever this was, it took his friend somewhere. And he wasn't sure he was coming back. And then Caleb would be alone. Alone in a dying town.

His chest grew tight, and his vision swam.

"I need you to understand that this is how things need to be," James said. "Anything else is just a pipe dream."

The metal food tray smacked into the side of James's head. Caleb looked at his own arm in disbelief.

James smiled. It wasn't real. It was a painted smile, a crease in a doll's plastic. A human smile was supposed to be more than a physical act. It was supposed to contain warmth.

This was ice with lips and teeth.

And blood was dripping down from the corner of James's mouth when he opened it to talk. A thick—already bruising—bite mark was on his tongue. He spoke around the filmy pink blood that dripped down his chin.

"It's okay; I used to believe in something, too."

Caleb couldn't help it. That was too much. He screamed and scrambled backward on the bed. The covers tangled around his feet. His hands came up to defend himself, hiding his face behind them.

"I suppose you'll be ready for surgery soon enough."

Caleb heard James move. He tensed even harder, whimpering. Part of his mind just wanted this all to stop. For whatever would happen to happen. Anything so he wasn't tightening around himself deeper and deeper.

But when he eventually lowered his arms, James was gone. The room was empty. The air didn't feel like it was dripping down his back, throat, and pores like rotten yolk.

His body kept shuddering. The ability to think past a spinning panic came slowly. Breathing normally again took intense effort. But he finally got somewhat calm.

Only this wasn't over. He was now in a hospital with something dangerous and supernatural happening around him. He looked at the door—at where Gabriel had gone.

On instinct, he picked up his phone—before remembering it didn't work. His hand clutched around it. He still tried calling the police. Once, twice, each time instantly getting no signal.

"Fuck you," he said, face screwing up in a panic. "Fuck this town."

Next, he tried the nurse call button. He hadn't used it since arriving in the hospital, but maybe it was still working, and someone, anyone else but James, would come to help. He pressed it once quickly. Then held it down.

It occurred to him that the faceless doctors might respond to it.

He stopped pressing, instead making a fist. And slammed it against the bedside.

Caleb was on the second story. He couldn't get outside help nearly fast enough. And he was pretty sure his friend was about to die.

Every atom of him wanted not to do what he was about to do. It was—*maybe*—safer to just sit in the room and hope that the monsters wouldn't come back.

After Caleb stood up, he couldn't get himself to move more. Standing there, committing to this plan even a little, took so much effort. He wanted to hide underneath the bed like he was a kid again.

It got worse when his eyes landed on the stain. A darkish liquid, vaguely blue, spread out from underneath where Gabriel had been sleeping.

He didn't want to pick up the blanket. Some part of him already knew it was something horrible. How could it not be?

But he reached out, hands shaking, pulsing with electricity. His heart rate radiated outward to the rest of his body in spikey bursts. The cloth was dry and awful between his fingers. He could drop it, go for the door, chase after his friend, but there was something clawing at his mind to be known.

He yanked it all at once, sending the fabric fluttering upward. And Caleb let out a small sound somewhere between a scream and a gasp. He didn't move, staring down at it. Whimpers trickled from his tight chest.

He'd been expecting weird blood, but this wasn't that. It wasn't one color but a myriad of hues: purple and cyan and deep, deeply crimson lines. It reminded him of an oil slick or graffiti drifting down a drain after he cleaned it off the Ink Well Diner's back wall. It was centralized in the middle of the bed, growing to a darker blue only at the edges.

It also looked like Gabriel's howling face.

Chapter Fifteen

THE FACE WAS DEFINITELY GABRIEL'S. Even with the jaw stretched and the eyes so wide they seemed to rise from the flat surface, he recognized it.

Now he noticed the slime had a smell. A cloyingly sweet stench that reminded him of burned sugar mixed with vinegar.

That finally got him to move. The door to the hallway made an awful squeak when he opened it, then it stopped abruptly and jolted his arm. It was like a rock was blocking its swing.

Or, as Caleb discovered when he squeezed around the opening, a little girl.

The girl tilted her head and smiled. She was missing a tooth right in the middle of her smile. She was shockingly pale, with hair that looked matted and stuck together. The girl wasn't tall, but she still somehow seemed towering.

"Where do *you* think you're going?" she asked.

Caleb opened his mouth, but no words made it past his lips. He floundered for another moment before defaulting to his usual response: apologizing.

"Sorry, are you okay?"

"Yes, why wouldn't I be?" the girl responded, her smile growing wider.

"I, uh… I don't know. I'm sorry, anyway… I need to go now."

Caleb took a step around her, only to meet another child standing directly out of his sightline. A little boy with curious eyes.

He also had a smile with a missing tooth.

"Where does the bug think he's going?" the boy asked. He put his hands on his hips.

"He's going after the surgeons. I bet his life," the girl replied.

Caleb shivered. The way they talked to each other felt staged. Each sentence had an undertone of malicious laughter.

"Where are your parents…?" he eventually asked.

"Hey, he didn't ask our names," the boy said. "That's a new one."

"Lucky, lucky," the girl replied.

Caleb's stomach dropped. More paranormal danger. Even if they looked like children, anxiety rolled along his spine and told him they were anything but. He tried not to react to it. It was like facing an angry animal: it might only chase you if you ran. He took a gentle step to go around the girl. Go toward where he assumed the surgeons took Gabriel.

Once he did, however, she stepped on top of his foot, shackling him to the spot. He looked down in alarm.

"You can't actually run from us," the girl said.

Her action was casual, with no noticeable strain, but it kept his leg still. Caleb's foot may as well have been part of the ground.

Before he could say anything, the boy grabbed his opposite hand. As soon as he touched him, there was an awful smell of ozone and blood. It crashed into his senses and made the world tilt toward vertigo.

And then the boy pulled. With the girl stopping his foot, he couldn't rebalance. She let him go just so he could topple. The fall sent pain through his temple and forced a shout from his lips. Once he'd blinked the stinging away, he swore and rubbed at his head.

"Please..."

He wasn't sure what he could ask. He imagined no request would elicit mercy.

"He did ask politely?" the girl asked. "Should we play along?"

"Nah," the boy said.

The two kids were standing next to each other. Only now did Caleb notice they wore the same outfit. A dull gray color.

"Let me help my friend..." was all Caleb could say.

"But you're going where you're not supposed to," the girl said. "It's not your turn yet."

"And we have some time to kill," the boy added.

They said the following words in perfect synch.

"*Or are you ready for surgery, too?*"

Caleb's eyes swam. It might've been a concussion, but they didn't look like children anymore. Not fully. Not when he squinted. They shifted like a heat shimmer. He waited for a demonic transformation, but the vision faded.

And they just watched.

"If you yell 'help' like we know you want to…" the girl began.

"Then we will show you what your brains look like," the boy finished.

"*Though everyone in Quill Point already knows what brains look like.*"

They cackled. It was a mix of the bubbling laughter of a child and something hissing and airy. It ended in a leveled-out screech like a radio signal failing.

Caleb got to his feet as fast as he could, sweating as he pushed himself up. His shoulder and back both spasmed, almost making him fall again. He gritted his teeth against it.

"*We'll give you credit. You got back up.*"

The kids stepped closer, and their faces were fake—plastic sheets covering something that drove static into his mind.

"*But we've yet to break you properly.*"

Caleb screamed. A burst of adrenaline sent him careening around them. The kids didn't move to intercept.

"Help! Someone!" he yelled, running down the hallway as best he could. Each motion made some part of him hurt.

As he ran, he could swear the hallway was elongating. The sound of his footfalls blended with a new aggressive hum from the fluorescent lights. He felt a rolling hatred from the two children, warping space in its wake.

"We don't hate you," the girl said. Her voice was sing-song and slightly too far away. "We're just finishing up something. Done this so many times now. We don't have any opinion of *you* at all."

"Except that you are insignificant and not worth remembering once we are done here," the boy chimed in gleefully.

"Well, yes, *that*, but it hardly makes *him* special."

He sharply looked back, almost throwing himself off balance. They walked casually together, going faster than possible.

"Running seems to be their defense mechanism," the boy said.

"Bugs, like I said. Ants try the same thing. They try to outrun a boot."

Caleb ran more. He panted, sweated, and refused to look back. Until panic settled in, and again, he glanced—

And they weren't there anymore.

The hallway was as it had been. Not changing, not warping. Empty. No strange hum anymore. And it was only as he stood there that it occurred to him how silent it all was. No one had come because of his screaming. No one investigated any of what had just happened.

A spike of nausea hit Caleb, but he kept it down. He could worry about human people later. The kids still had to be around. There weren't any doors for them to have disappeared through—unless they'd doubled back. They just *weren't* anymore. They'd let him go. And that made Caleb even more nervous than he'd been before.

His shuddering breath came out in pulses, but he moved again. He was going to the main surgery room. He half-expected the wall signs not to read correctly anymore, but navigation was easy. Silent and easy.

Every few moments, Caleb expected them to jump out at him. But nothing came. No bang, no screech.

A sound did eventually break the stalemate. A slithering entered earshot as he rounded a corner, and he caught

Gabriel being dragged across the floor. His eyes were still empty, and the surgeons pulled him without effort.

"Hey!" Caleb yelled, chasing after them.

Gabriel regarded him silently. His mouth slack, and his blinks languid. Caleb was almost sure he was catatonic, but as the doors to the surgery room swung open, he gave this little wave goodbye.

The door swung closed with a slight pop.

Caleb managed one more burst of speed. He slammed into the door, then pounded on it repeatedly. It hurt, but he didn't stop.

"Please! H-he doesn't want this!"

The door opened a crack. A face without coherent features looked back at him.

"*Does that matter?*"

"Please... he's my friend..."

"*We can't. What kind of precedent would that set? It wouldn't be fair to everyone else.*"

Caleb pushed on the door. It did nothing. It was like trying to move a brick wall by hand.

"*He should've planned better.*"

The face slipped back inside, and the door started to close. Without thinking, Caleb shoved his foot into the gap. The pain was immediately too harsh for words. Multiple bones audibly snapped.

Caleb howled in pain. He pulled his foot back and stumbled into the wall. The back of his head smacked into it, and he saw white. Then he slid against the wall into a heap.

"Gabriel," he said around tears. He clutched his leg, not daring to touch the toes.

Gabriel spoke, but not to him. His voice came clearer than it should have—unknown means amplified it.

"How long will this take?" Gabriel asked.

"*Only a few minutes.*"

"*This is rather routine. We've done this a lot today.*"

Caleb shuddered, trying to form thoughts. The pain was numbing everything else, derailing any focus.

Gabriel said his following words with such a gentle sadness—soft and vulnerable and close to tears. It sounded like Caleb's friend again, not the hollow thing he'd woken up to before.

"Will things get better?"

The answer was something Caleb had never heard. It simply didn't have an equivalent to draw from. A thick tearing. A violent noise wet with clinging fibers and the expulsion of fluid.

A smell more pungent than rotting sunbaked garbage slammed into Caleb's nose and coated his tongue too fast to shut his mouth. Rancid bile instantly flooded up his throat.

Then came a sound that Caleb knew. He knew it on a primal level. He knew it as every living thing does.

"No… no, *please*… fucking *stop*… please…"

A mixture. Raw and throat-tearing. Screaming and crying in pain ruptured out from that door. It rattled the very air.

Caleb cupped his hands over his ears to block it out. Any of it reaching his mind made him see red—a rending feeling between the eyes and across his skull.

But he could hear it despite his efforts. He experienced that panting, agonized procession. The cacophony of pleading and begging, and, "I can't," and, "kill me," and, "I'm so sorry," and, "Mom," and—

Tears streaming down his face and his frame shaking, Caleb pulled himself across the floor—pulled himself away. The suffering followed and assaulted his ears, getting somehow louder. Somehow only sounding worse and worse.

Nothing could be alive after those sounds.

"I'm sorry," was all Caleb could think to say as he abandoned Gabriel.

Eventually, he stood. Leaning on the wall as best he could and, using the heel of his damaged foot when he had to, he staggered away. The pain of moving was nothing compared to that of staying nearby. Adrenaline numbed the physical pain.

"Please make it stop!" Gabriel howled.

Caleb's lip quivered, and more tears, more chest quaking sobs overwhelmed his senses. But he kept running away.

The screaming fell silent—an abrupt stoppage of all sounds. Caleb couldn't help but imagine his friend having his throat slit.

"I'm so sorry," Caleb said to no one. And then pushed through the double doors into the hospital's reception area.

Chapter Sixteen

When the door closed behind him, his ears popped. It felt like entering another dimension where the air molecules didn't move at the same rate.

The otherwise normalcy was the more striking thing, however: bucket seats, tinny music, a little television playing nothing. The reception desk had no one behind it, but looked otherwise mundane. It was as if the receptionist had simply stepped away, past a nondescript door behind the desk. The water cooler burbled slightly, sounding almost pleased to see him.

Across the room, the doorway out was simply there. On the other side was a parking lot on a hill, unless reality was gone. He wouldn't put it past it.

Caleb looked back at the doors he had entered through. Nothing chased after him. Nothing was coming for him. His friend had died, and now he could leave. He went for the exit.

It felt like a trick. He pushed on the exit, and it didn't open—but it was just because the deadbolt was sealed. A typical piece of metal held it closed.

Caleb looked back again. Still nothing.

He leaned against the door and tugged on the deadbolt. His fingers slipped off it. It felt greased with butter. Or melted fat. Its surface wasn't shiny, but it was slippery to a degree only ice or lubricant could manage.

With increasing frustration, he tugged. He'd been doing that for almost a minute when the smell hit. Burning sugar mixed with vinegar—a reek growing in pungency.

A bubble formed at the door's hinge, and Caleb pulled back just in time to not get splashed. Popping with increasingly sized bursts of snotty liquid was that cyan, red, and purple slime that had been on Gabriel's bed.

It pooled remarkably quickly. Before he could stumble away, it touched the edge of his foot. The slime was only slightly colder than room temperature.

It swirled wherever it lay. The swirls were making faces. Faces of people in the town. Some he even recalled as customers at the diner. Fuck, even his old landlord and usual hairstylist. Elongated and distended suffering painted itself around him.

The image of something in that slime pulling him down, of a hand bursting forth, slid into his mind, and he stumbled backward faster. Caleb kept wincing as he put too much weight on his damaged foot. The toes were already turning various colors. Harsh swears trickled from his throat when he stepped down wrong.

The slime did nothing more than slowly get bigger, however. It didn't chase him. It was a gently flowing, macabre oil slick. He watched it continue flowing from the door. Within less than thirty seconds, the wood, the handle, the surrounding wall, and much of the carpet were slick with that frictionless slime.

The water cooler burbled again, and that broke the spell. Caleb looked away, grinding his teeth. The front door wouldn't work—and the monster children not attacking him now didn't mean they weren't nearby.

As if on cue, he heard their voices faintly down the hall. He couldn't quite tell what they were saying.

Caleb's mind was running far too fast, and it was hard to hold a thought past an immediate reaction. He clutched his forehead, trying to push past all the internal noise. He didn't know the whole layout of the hospital, and he didn't know where another exit door was.

But anywhere was better than staying here.

He hurried to the side of the receptionist's desk. There was a door to get into that workspace—and then he could get to the door behind the desk. He tugged down the door handle. It was locked. He tugged it twice more, seeing if he could loosen it. The mechanism could be old.

It didn't budge much, only slightly dipping lower than before. He could break through it if he had more time or a tool.

The children's voices grew more audible.

"He seems almost ready," the little boy said.

Caleb swallowed any outward reaction. They might not know *exactly* where he was—assuming the slime wasn't directly their doing. With how much his body hurt from all this sudden exertion, he wasn't sure how much more running he could do. He needed to focus on staying just ahead of them until he found another exit.

As quietly as possible and using all the strength he had left in his arms, he pulled himself over the hard and uncomfortable desktop. Trying for a slow descent, he wriggled his body to the edge, knocking loose staplers and rolls of tape.

There was nothing for this last part. He let gravity do its work. The carpet was not as soft as he would've liked and tasted like dust and dirt.

"See, do you sense that?" said the little boy somewhere nearby.

"I detect human," the girl responded. "This whole town reeks of it."

"Underneath that," the boy said. "He's getting there, now."

"And you're sure this is the last one we need?"

"Well, yes, but not the last one we can hurt."

The girl let out that laugh again. That laugh that screeched.

"Oh, I do so *like* the sound of that."

"I thought you might, Sister."

Caleb used the nearby chair to pull himself up. Forcing himself to breathe past a bout of lightheadedness, he opened the door behind the desk and stepped into the dark.

His eyes adjusted easily enough. It was a series of rooms connected by archway entrances. Filing cabinets taller than him stood shiny and solid. It was probably where they stored patient files. Quill Point was old enough a town not to have gone totally digital yet.

He couldn't hear the children anymore. That alone propelled him forward, gritting his teeth as he did so. After passing through several archways and flinching from random shadows in the cluttered rooms, he slowed down. Focusing on simply going forward.

It was getting harder. Adrenaline was wearing off. His knee burned from how often he had to hold up his obliterated foot. That tumble over the desk had agitated his shoulder and neck. And his foot—well, he was trying hard to ignore it.

A glance back toward the shut door confirmed they hadn't followed him. Unless they could also pass through walls or be completely silent.

After passing one more archway and rounding a slight corner, he came to another door. It had a lock, but fortunately, he was on the right side to turn it. He turned it gingerly. The sound was still a gunshot in that stagnant space.

He let out a single breath, flinched when Gabriel's last words flickered through his head, then opened the door.

Chapter Seventeen

He was back in the main hallway. Gone in a thin circle. To the right of him was where he had heard the children before. To the right was the slime and the faces.

He went left.

A building with two stories surely had to have exits on both sides. It would violate some building code or firefighter's rule to not have another way out.

Immediately, the hallway didn't feel right. Within a few steps, it was obvious. The air wasn't the same. It was cold and moving in swaying currents, spinning around him, like standing between dust devils full of invisible leaves. The lights above gradually hummed louder and louder and glowed the wrong color. It made the hallway the hues of drunken evenings.

In the corner of his eye, every time he moved, an after-image of himself blurred. He waved his hand and watched a grainy version of it languidly follow, slightly out of sync.

Caleb looked up at the clock, and it had hundreds of hands, all overlapping and moving in layers. The second hands were marching lines—ants crawling in rows. It made his eyes hurt.

When he swore out loud, it sounded somehow both underwater and in an echoing cave.

"Fucking... fuck... lost... losing..."

Pockets of air crystalized for fleeting moments, revealing people. Lots of them, actually. Shadow people, solid people, blurry people milled around him. Some called out in alarm—in that same hard-to-hear way—asking where someone was. Others walked in pensive loneliness. Still more dully looked at nothing, the glint gone like Gabriel's.

They always took a path that Caleb didn't—missing him like they were both positively charged magnets. Until one walked through him, going in the opposite direction. And in a rush of cold clarity, they were together.

"Hey!" Caleb yelled.

The man spun around. "Huh..."

"Are you real?" Caleb asked.

The man looked middle-aged, with white skin, brown eyes, and mild acne scars. He wore a shirt for some pet store Caleb recognized from around Quill Point.

"Of course I'm real. I... do you know what's going on? I was getting treated for a bite, and then..."

Caleb sputtered for a second, trying to talk. "You need to get out of... out of h-here. Something is happening. Like with the sky..."

The man blurred away. His response was tinny and disappeared into the cacophony of other shadows' panicked cries. The crowd grew fuller—the thin hallway stuffed to bursting, and the man's silhouette faded into the crowd.

Even with Caleb's panicked, exhausted mental state, he jolted with understanding. The hospital wasn't empty. It had never been. The people were still here.

They were all here.

"Can anyone hear me?!" he shouted. He ran up to another shadow, but they skirted away. "Please... there's something wrong..."

A door clicked—a door that looked much more solid than anything else in the hallway. And Caleb tensed. For a second, surrounded by so many others, he'd forgotten that he was being hunted.

The door opened slightly, and a pair of tired eyes looked out at him. They were much too high up on the doorframe to belong to the kids, but they also didn't belong to anyone he knew.

"Please be quiet. There's no point in being loud," the person said.

"Wait, can you see me—"

Whomever it was closed the door with a weary sigh.

Caleb looked at the door. He'd not had a great deal of luck going through doors. Or following people.

Through the din of the shadow-crowd was giggling in stereo.

Caleb froze and looked behind him.

Through the smog of people, the smoke, the flowing forms, two things were moving toward him at a leisurely pace.

Skipping, to be exact.

"We know you're nearby," the little girl called out. "You can run all you want."

The door didn't seem so bad to Caleb anymore. He opened it as quietly as he could and slid through. The sound of so many shadow people chattering was dulled by the wall.

Caleb looked around. It was so dark. Even worse than the archives. The windows were mostly covered by curtains, but through the cracks, they were coated over with something. It glowed from what light got through.

The room itself consisted of a bunch of tables and a few countertops around the edges. It had that faint smell of dried crumbs and coffee left out for too long.

"They're so loud," said that same voice.

Caleb looked in the voice's general direction but saw nothing. He wasn't sure he wanted to. The voice sounded squeezed, pushed out.

Instead, he focused on the first good sign in a long time. Windows. Windows meant an exit—even if it meant climbing down somehow. Gently, oh so gently, he went for them.

Caleb's heart was absolutely *pounding* in his chest.

"Is someone there?" the voice whispered. "I hear footsteps?"

Caleb froze. His throat practically closed. Now he knew where the person—if they were a person—was sitting. Over in the corner. That patch, the person-shaped silhouette.

"I suppose it doesn't matter," the voice said.

Caleb nodded in agreement. There was no reason to pay attention to what he was doing. They could ignore each other. He breathed as quietly as he could.

Caleb reached the windows and brushed back the curtains. Hopefully, he wasn't letting in enough light to bother whatever was sitting in the room with him. He used his nails to scrape away part of whatever was coating the glass. Only after some of it was underneath his fingernails did he understand what it was.

The fine misting of hair and the visible blue veins tipped him off.

Vomit wanted out, and it barely didn't escape. Shallow breaths were about all Caleb could muster. He looked away but still tore off a bigger section. The sound wasn't like tearing paper.

"Oh, light," said the voice.

Caleb looked over again at the person sitting there. They hadn't stood or moved from their spot, and their voice didn't even sound annoyed.

"I see you trying over there. There's nothing out *there* that's worth anything," the person continued quietly. "Not in Quill Point. The citizens don't matter. We all don't. The world's going to end."

Caleb gritted his teeth and tore more. If the person knew he was in the room, being quiet wasn't necessary. The children could arrive any second. If he could get to the shutters—

The shutters opened with a faint pop, letting in air. Blissful fucking air. But the windowpane only went a few inches up. Not even enough to get his entire arm through.

Caleb ducked slightly to look through the hole. Down below sat a row of abandoned, dead cars. They were still there from when Murder Sky somehow rendered them all immovable.

Caleb tilted his gaze a bit. As expected, he'd need to climb down, and it would require shattering the glass and then risk dropping an entire story to the ground. The bushes below weren't the bounciest looking plants, but at least there was something besides the parking lot's blacktop.

"No one is coming to save you," the figure said.

Caleb turned his head, and for a second, he almost wanted to yell. Or cry. He *knew* that. God-fucking-dammit, he knew that.

"But I have to try everything," Caleb said. He sighed, then said it again quietly. He whispered it for *himself*.

"You really don't. I tried to leave. I wasn't even supposed to be here. I live in a different state. I was just visiting my parents. But my car wasn't working, so I got stuck in this town. But it was always going to be like this, no matter what I did. There's no point in denying what's come for the world."

"I'm going to break this window. You stay there."

"That's fine."

Caleb walked over to the table. Glanced at the door. The children hadn't found him yet.

"If you're thinking about the siblings, they're probably about to find you. They probably already know where you are and what you're doing. They drag it out," the figure informed him.

Caleb looked at the figure again. There was enough light to see them somewhat. They were sitting. They were stooped over in their chair, folded in on themselves, and were looking down at the ground. It was almost like their knees had disappeared into their stomach. Their hair was black and long.

"W-who are you?"

"My name is Albert. But it doesn't matter."

"I'm sure it does matter," Caleb found himself saying. He hated platitudes when others used them on him. But faced with all *this*, they were all he could think to say.

"We'll be the same," Albert said, then shook his head gently, making his black hair sway.

"I'm sorry for whatever happened to you."

"Ha," he replied flatly.

Caleb frowned, then tried to pick up the chair. It was heavy, and it needed a running attack for what he was going to do.

Caleb knew this would hurt like nothing else in the entire universe. But he leaned against the chair, set his injured foot gently to the ground, and hyped himself up for it.

"One time," he said.

"It's not going to work," Albert said. "But you can waste time however you want to."

The spike of annoyance came again—but this time had a worthwhile function. It burned in him. He'd been hopeless for so fucking long. Worried about making rent, worried about the future. And every action, even the positive ones, was so tied to anxious worry; it felt like dragging a weight. Every decision took mental strength.

But this would be primal, and there was no second chance.

Caleb planted his broken foot, and before the pain could send him to the floor, he pushed off. He flung himself forward, carrying the chair high above his head. He roared, screamed, and cursed in one guttural utterance.

Caleb brought the chair down in a furious arc, letting it out of his grip at the peak of its momentum. He collapsed as it finished its flight.

The chair bounced off the glass, leaving a spiderweb of damage and sending the wood crashing to the ground. The chair broke into jagged shards, spilling pieces of wood across the floor.

One skidded right in front of Caleb as tears streamed down his face. His mouth hung open.

"See, I told you," Albert said.

A vibrational rush of air rippled through the room. A beast's roar made everything shake. Even as the sound became quieter, softer, and then finalized as childlike giggling, the entire room rumbled.

"*We heard you!*" came the singsong duet.

Caleb couldn't help but scream.

Chapter Eighteen

In the dark, he scrambled with his knees. Everything hurt. Survival was the only focus. Everything *fucking* hurt. He had to find an option. Something in this room.

A small closet fell into view. It was against the wall. It was silver and had a grate at both the top and bottom of its door. He shuffled toward it, keeping down whimpers that escaped his mouth.

"They'll find you," Albert announced.

Caleb didn't even acknowledge him. He crawled to it—then nearly toppled over while stretching to yank the door open. The closet was spacious, with a metal bottom and a small bevy of hospital scrubs hanging above. He crawled underneath the scrubs and made his body as small as possible.

Through the lower grate, he could see into the room, even if it was full of shadows.

But when the children entered, he wasn't sure whether what he saw was real.

It was like staring at CGI or a hyper-realistic video game—some part of the brain simply wouldn't accept the visual.

It was a pair of creatures, each taller than him. Almost taller than the ceiling.

The one on the left was gray. Thin and gliding with a slightly too-smooth motion. The skin was rippling, shifting with some unseen force underneath. Almost like bugs were crawling in straight lines.

The other, on the right, was like a cloud in a humanoid shape, with patches of sporadic darkness signaling thunder. A series of hands, with long fingers and sharp nails, waved along its skin in undulating rows like seaweed underwater.

They spoke with the voices of the little kids.

"I think he's practically there," the clay monster said. It had the little girl's voice. "It's so inefficient to do things this way. I had that whole hotel in an hour, at most."

"Yes," the little boy replied, "but Father does know best."

"Question, Brother, does a bug know what it is before a human smashes it?"

"I don't know. Maybe we should *ask*."

Caleb shrank back even further. He waited for them to tear him apart, to open up his head like the people around the Prayer Spire.

But he slowly realized they were not talking about him.

"How was surgery, Albert?" the little boy asked.

"It was what it was," Albert responded. "I was ready for it."

"Do you remember me?"

"Does it matter?"

"No, *you* don't. But it was nice to be feared the way you did. All the other little scrambling bugs trying just to avoid my hands, not realizing I had the whole town in my grasp."

"You were the sky?"

The girl giggled. "Oh, he's much more than a human sky. You couldn't conceive of what we are."

"But you wouldn't want to," the little boy said. "Would you, Albert?"

"Nothing has mattered since you showed up. I saw the Spire, I got my surgery, and it didn't matter."

"Oh, the Spire matters," the girl said. "The Spire matters a whole lot. But we don't explain things to insignificant beings. Brother, are we done with him now?"

"I suppose so," the boy said gleefully. "We've already gotten what we need from you."

"Are you going to kill me?" Albert asked.

"*Would you care if we did?*"

"No."

Caleb just barely had the presence of mind to cover his ears. It didn't help.

An awful keening laugh in stereo came, and then the sound of a blade against a rock. A scratching sound that grew wetter and wetter. A chainsaw into flesh or through a brain.

Albert didn't make a sound.

Caleb shut his eyes tight. The noises faded away, and the silence was all there was. But he knew where they were. No way had they simply left.

He opened his eyes, and they stood on either side of Albert, facing away, looking at the closet. Albert was still moving, apparently alive, but only his face was distinguishable anymore. The rest was red and pink and bone and blissfully hard to discern beyond that.

Caleb could easily see the monsters' mouths now. A gaping maw of pure darkness, ready to engulf a whole person. A clay-like extended smile, longer than a person is wide, with squirming things between tombstone teeth.

"I can hear you think, Caleb," the little girl said. "I could hear it the whole time."

Caleb stifled a scream. His heart rate slammed into his chest. At the edge of his vision, he could see something squirming.

"I could hear you every night since I've been here. Your mind spinning like a pottery wheel. Wondering how things will turn out. Desperately wanting someone to tell you how it will all be okay."

It was cloudy in Caleb's thoughts. His chest hurt, and his stomach was swirling with sickness. Something was *pushing* into his mind, and it squeezed his skull as it did.

"Oh, but here's the thing, Caleb. I can tell you the truth. You will *never* succeed. You aren't special. When you look at the news and hear about someone facing bankruptcy, facing financial ruin, and think, 'no, that will never happen to me,' you're deluding yourself. There's no magic escape. You will never own anything you want, always just renting what meager things others deem worthy of profit. You will never see a life built. The future will be nothing but the toil to earn enough to not die. And when you feel like it's all hopeless, you'll still be in debt. And when you wither away, you'll pass it on to whoever has to pay for your *fucking funeral*."

A shudder passed through Caleb, and whatever it was that was pressing in finally burst. In his mind's eye, he could see flowing watercolor. Pastels taking shape and form.

He thought of the house he'd wanted. A two-floor, four-bedroom, with a library of books he'd enjoy—once he had time to read again. An office where he could make a business for himself. A beautiful lawn he could mow every Sunday.

Oh, he could see it.

And a wife! One day, he would have enough time to find someone. One day have enough money to give her beautiful things and go on the dates she deserved. Have kids together and give them the best education.

He could hear them laughing and playing.

And then a retirement. After many years of good work, he could retire. He and his wife could go somewhere beautiful and see chunks of the world at a pace where the majesties weren't postcards and search results.

The painting grew splotchy—lines of it melted down the canvas in his mind. He had no way to grasp it, but it would've shifted away even if he did. It became unrecognizable.

Nausea surged in him with such force. Tears splashed down his cheeks, thicker than they should be. His hands went to his eyes and came away with multicolored slime. Cyan, red, and purple slime.

Another surge made his back go ramrod straight. The tears came faster than any tears ever could. They formed rivers down his cheeks. Like bursting pustules, the fluid abandoned him.

The door to the small closet swung open, and the fluid formed puddles across the floor. Forming in slow motion, in shifts and segments, his face.

Caleb looked down at a painting of himself. And felt nothing about it at all.

"I'm ready for surgery," he said.

Chapter Nineteen

THE TWO MEN WITHOUT FACES PINNED him to a surgical bed stained with a greater variety of fluids than he thought the body could produce.

"*We just need to prepare you a little*," one said and dabbed at his forehead with a cloth that smelled like alcohol.

"*Just a routine procedure*," the other chimed in, taking a pair of scissors from his pocket and cutting at the lower hem of his shirt.

The cut went straight up, exposing his stomach. Caleb looked at it with dull eyes.

"Thanks," he said.

"*All in day's work*."

"It's almost time," the little girl said cheerfully.

Caleb looked over at her. The girl and her brother were standing on either side of Brianna. They both looked like their little kid forms again.

Brianna looked different than he'd last seen her. Her skin was pale and sickly, and she had bags underneath her eyes. She had also gotten dangerously thin, drowning in her colorful shirt. She didn't seem aware of what was happening around her.

"Are you excited?" the little girl asked.

"No, I just don't care what you do to me," Caleb answered.

"Good answer," the little boy said.

"*Almost time now. We will begin momentarily. Please refrain from unneeded twitching, screaming, or pleading. It doesn't matter.*"

Caleb nodded his agreement.

"*We will be using you for one of the most important parts of the process. We will allow you the majesty of all your organs going to use, but your spine will allow him to fully materialize on a Layer. You should be honored. He is almost complete because of people like you.*"

Caleb didn't know who "he" was, but the figure popped into view as soon as the faceless man said it. Reality slid an inch, and the figure was as clear as anything in the world could be.

He sat on a throne of gold. A huge structure of bones covered in liquid metal. The throne glowed with a nuclear light.

He was larger than any human and had no skin. A glorious scaffolding of femurs and collarbones formed impenetrable armor. His insides were held in place by crisscrossing ligaments. An interlocking mound of segmented livers, deflated stomach, still-beating hearts, and eyeball pulp formed its bulk, gently throbbing with tributaries of cyan, purple, and crimson blood. His eyes were many mortal eyes, stitched together from sclera to sclera.

And though the eyes remained dark for now, a light that could melt skin grew in intensity from deep inside.

"*He is The Lethal Lies.*"

A hum that shook the air grew with each word spoken.

"*Without him, we are dust.*"

"He is The Stolen Dreams," the little girl said.

The light in those unearthly amalgam eyes pulsed with starlight and solar explosions.

The little boy chimed in, "He is The Unfulfilled Promises."

Bree's mouth slowly opened. Her voice, pained and dry, forced itself from her throat.

"He is … The God of Greed."

The citizens of Quill Point will return.
At least, the ones who are still alive.

Book Club Questions

1. Quill Point had a widely known plan in case of a disaster. Do you think it was a good plan, given what the characters knew of the situation? What would you have made the plan if you could've changed it?
2. When Albert's mom argues that it's not his responsibility to help, he says, "No, it's not my responsibility. But I'm part of the problem if I think like that." Do you agree with that argument? Do you think Albert was right to go?
3. Charley makes several quick decisions and actions once he understands what's happening. What would be the first thing you'd do if faced with a similar event?
4. Bree has strong opinions about art and about art persisting past its creator. Do you agree with her? If you don't, what do you think Bree is wrong about?
5. Milda states that horror can have a calming effect in certain cases. Do you find this to be true? Why or why not? What type of media would you go to if you needed to calm yourself during a scary time?
6. The little girl posits all humans want immortality. Do you agree with her? Why or why not would you want to be immortal?
7. The little girl says to Bree, "This way, you're only complicit by inaction. By association. Your favorite." Do you agree Bree is guilty of something by association or inaction?

8. The Mayor of Quill Point misuses his power and influence several times toward evil means. What systems or circumstances allow someone like that to come to power and keep it for so long?
9. Caleb is deeply afraid of medical debt and concerned about his financial future. Do you think his worries were justified?
10. Several characters use nihilistic rhetoric while under the sway of supernatural magic. How much of what they say do you think were their already held beliefs, and how much was instigated by the supernatural?
11. The God of Greed is given several other names, such as "The Lethal Lies" and "The Unfulfilled Promises." What do you think these names communicate about the nature of greed? Do you agree with them?
12. *Nothing Will Be Left* covers several themes, including greed, political corruption, debt, and poverty. How do you think these themes were handled? What scenes effectively communicated these themes, and what scenes missed the mark?

Author Bio

October Kane is a horror writer and an avid horror fan, primarily found wandering in Florida. Since a ridiculously young age, he's enjoyed trying to come up with creative monsters, and after discovering that drawing them would never be his strong suit, he found a deep love for writing. Since then, he's focused on describing those monsters as vividly and gruesomely as possible. His love of cosmic horror happened much later, but it quickly became his favorite of the subgenres for its creative freedom and focus on existential themes.

When October Kane isn't working on his novels or other creative projects, he enjoys horror movies, terrifying podcasts, and all kinds of scary books, which surely has nothing to do with him being practically nocturnal. You can find out more about him online at www.octoberkane.com.

More books from 4 Horsemen Publications

Horror, Thriller, & Suspense

Alan Berkshire
Jungle
Hell's Road

Erika Lance
Jimmy
Illusions of Happiness
No Place for Happiness
I Hunt You

Maria DeVivo
Witch of the Black Circle
Witch of the Red Thorn
Witch of the Silver Locust

Mark Tarrant
The Mighty Hook

Steve Altier
The Ghost Hunter

Ingram Content Group UK Ltd.
Milton Keynes UK
UKHW011837070723
424723UK00004B/197